THE RUMBALL RUMBA: A DICKENS HOLIDAY ROMANCE

First edition. November 23, 2021.

Copyright © 2021 Bonnie Edwards.

ISBN: 978-1989226148

Written by Bonnie Edwards

Table of Contents

For all of us who love the magic of Christmas, old and young alike.

For Ted, always.

What readers like you have said about
The Tinsel Tango, A Dickens Holiday Novella

5 Stars!
"I love this story and I love spending time in Dickens"
5 Stars!
"...another wonderful, sweet romance."
5 Stars!
"Well written with great characters. I'm looking forward to the next installment in this author's holiday stories"
5 Stars!
"Edwards's characters touch your heart and tickle your funny bone."

The Rumball Rumba
A Dickens Holiday Romance
By
Bonnie Edwards

Chapter One

July 3 – Dickens

"I'm getting a divorce." Those words had seemed like a dreadful announcement to give her family last Christmas, but she'd weathered the storm. The combined Moore and James families had rallied quickly and supported her through the whole messy business. Dale, her husband of too many years, had left her for his much younger receptionist.

It still pinched that she was the first divorcee in her family. Trix Warden, loser at marriage. Last Christmas she couldn't imagine anything worse.

Until now, today.

Because today she got to say the words, "I'm pregnant. I'm a pregnant divorcee." She winced because that wasn't the worst of it.

She smoothed her flowy white blouse and denim shorts as she walked the hall in Gram's house.

Everyone had gathered for the Fourth of July weekend. From the kitchen she saw them on the patio, sitting on chairs in a semi-circle, cold drinks in hand. Her cousins Kayley and Brenna sat beside Brenna's husband, Jett. He wore his usual expression; besotted. Not only did he love her cousin he was wealthy and generous. Kind, too. They'd only been married a few months having met right here in Dickens last Christmas.

She'd overshadowed their budding romance with her horrid divorce announcement, but that couldn't be helped.

She sucked in her belly and plastered on a smile. Her Egyptian cotton top was long and roomy. It was perfect for July heat. This morning, without warning, she'd been unable to zip up her best pair of shorts. She'd had to dig through her 'big' clothes and cut off her pre-divorce jeans above the knee. Her blossoming tummy needed more room.

Trix drew in a breath and slid open the screen slider. "Hi everyone. I made it. Getting out of Brooklyn was a bear."

Her mother, Laurel, known to the family as Lolly, was first to reach her. Trix hugged her harder than usual and her mom gave her a curious glance as she stepped back to give Brenna and Kayley room to enfold her.

Next came hugs from her Aunt Jennifer and Uncle Reggie and then, a brief hug and pat on the back from Jett. Gram rose from her seat and Trix walked to her. Gram smelled of roses and kindness and Trix held on for a long moment. She hoped her grandmother wouldn't be disappointed in her, but that, too, couldn't be helped.

After more discussion about traffic, everyone's health and jobs, the announcement loomed heavily in her heart.

When Brenna passed her a glass of wine, Trix raised her palm to give the drink a pass. "I'll have some of Gram's famous punch." Non-alcoholic, the punch was fruity, light, and delicious and none of the younger generation chose it on arrival.

Brenna cocked an inquiring eyebrow but smiled. "More for the rest of us."

"Good, because you'll need it," Trix stated clearly. When everyone turned their gazes to her, she swallowed. "I'm pregnant."

She couldn't help a tremulous smile from escaping. They'd love the pregnant part, of course. But not the rest of her story.

Shock moved across their faces like a brushstroke across canvas, slapping each of them as the words sunk in. She and Dale had tried to get pregnant for years. He'd blamed her and when he got his receptionist pregnant, he'd been triumphant as he'd demanded a divorce.

Before any of the family could speak, she said what she'd come here to say. "By Dale."

Jett looked confused and leaned into Brenna's ear. "Her cheating ex-husband, Dale?"

"That's right, Jett." Trix straightened her shoulders and looked at her mom. Laurel stared back as she calculated dates. Trix braced for the fallout.

"How? And when? You're not even showing. He left you over seven months ago." She bit her lip. "Oh, baby, you..." her words trailed off.

"It was a last hurrah. A final goodbye." A desperate night where they'd both been lonely and longing for connection. She, because Brenna and Jett had married that day and Trix had felt incredibly old and alone as she'd watched the bride and groom, delirious with joy. Dale, because the young woman he'd left Trix for had lost their baby and he was overcome with grief.

"No, it was more than a goodbye," she began. "Marie, Dale's wife, lost their baby, and he came to me, grieving, shaking with tears. He wanted to say he was sorry for what he'd done to me and to our marriage. But when I opened the door to him, all I saw were the years we'd hoped in vain for a baby of our own."

"Pity sex," Kayley said, sounding sage.

"Comfort sex," her mom said with a soft sigh. "We've all been there."

Jennifer stood and came to her. "Sex with the ex is common enough and you don't need to explain yourself."

"The final goodbye came in the morning when he told me he never wanted to see me again. Never wanted to be reminded of our marriage or what he did to it. As far as he was concerned, he'd made a terrible mistake and went home to his wife." She shrugged. She'd been happy to see the back of him. Good riddance.

"Oh, Trix. You haven't told him about the baby?" Her grandmother was a discerning woman and could see past the surface.

She shook her head. Her decision had been made weeks ago when she called Dale one last time. Before she could tell him, he'd given her his news. "They're expecting again and have now moved to Oregon to live near her parents." She blew out a big breath. "Dale's gone and I'm here. I don't need child support, except for the family kind and I'd never get that from Dale. Not now."

Gram rose from her chair and took Trix's hands. When she faced her grandmother, the older woman smiled, her face alive with joy. "And you'll have all the support you need. A baby's on the way; a baby we'll all love and cherish, just as we love and cherish you."

Trix's eyes flooded, and tears streamed. She nodded and swiped the sudden wet. "I—all I know for sure—is I want to live here. Have the baby in Dickens and raise it surrounded by family."

"You'll live here with me," Gram said. "There's loads of room."

Trix looked at her mom. Laurel nodded. "For a while, at least. When will you move?"

"I have to sell my place, get a business plan together, find a location for a gallery and tons of other things." She had a to-do list a mile long.

Kayley snorted. "Take that, Dale. He never supported your art or your dreams."

It was true. And after he left her, she'd proved him wrong. A wonderful gallery, *De Rigueur*, famous for fostering new talent had taken three of her paintings and given her back her ambition. Those brightly colored portraits had sold quickly and Trix had stepped into a career and a future she'd only dreamed about.

October 31 – Dickens
          "This place is perfect," Trix said as she wandered through old Mr. Scott's new barn. The widower had passed away, leaving his home and property with several years of unpaid taxes. His only son had come

to bury his father and had taken what he wanted from the property. The horse barn stood empty and had never been used.

The house had been sold last month, but the barn was on a different lot so was still available for a price a soon-to-be single mom could afford. She was cutting it to the wire, but with the right help she may have her business up and running before the real Christmas rush began. Finding the right help was crucial. She needed a contractor who could move mountains, handle setbacks, and stay on budget. She'd watched enough renovations shows on television to understand setbacks were common.

After her promising start at *De Rigueur*, sales of her paintings had grown exponentially. Word of mouth was a wonderful thing. By early September, she'd sold her tiny apartment and moved in with Gram. She'd been looking for the perfect location for her gallery and market ever since.

Her plan was to focus on her business for now and get her own place to live when the baby needed more space. Gram wasn't lonely with Trix there.

Thanks to Dale's mocking and dismissive comments about her painting, Trix understood that an artist needed money. While he'd berated her for her taking time for her 'ridiculous' hobby, he'd instilled an understanding that if she ever returned to her easel, she'd need to have a solid financial plan.

This barn would give her exactly what she wanted. She'd continue with *De Rigueur* but have this gallery, too. If her plan came together, she'd have income from her sales, a modest percentage of the other artists' sales and their rent. Dale would be proud. Hah...no, he'd say it still wasn't good enough, because nothing ever was for him.

She smoothed a hand across her burgeoning belly and smiled.

"How many booths do you see in this space?" Her cousin Brenna asked as Jett wandered around shaking beams and kicking at the concrete floor. "How many do you need to make a living?"

"I'll start with ten. And leave space between for expansion if the artists want or need more room."

"Do you have agreements in place already?" Jett asked. He was a businessman and a good sounding board.

"I have pledges of interest, but without a building to show them, I couldn't expect to sign anyone." She'd been all over the state looking for weavers, potters, glass blowers, and more. She'd struck gold when she'd suggested rents would go down if they brought in other artists. Now, people were coming to her. She tried to tamp down her excitement, but it overflowed, and surely showed on her face. "I want this place up and running before the Christmas rush."

Jon Carpenter parked his truck outside the Scott barn. He'd put weeks into getting the barn ready for horses. He'd basically rebuilt it from the ground up, including pouring the concrete floor. Old man Scott had paid good money and on time, but never did bring in any horses. He'd become too ill to fulfill his dream. A shame because the barn had stood empty. Now the house had been sold and the barn had less appeal to buyers. Who would want a barn without a house?

Jon knocked once on the entrance door to announce his arrival and then stepped inside. Three people looked over expectantly. He saw a couple obviously connected since they were holding hands and a pregnant woman who stood near them. Her expression was hopeful, excited, and happy.

"Mr. Carpenter?" She asked with some eagerness. "I'm Trix Warden."

He nodded. "Mrs. Warden. Nice to meet you," he greeted her. She was a pretty thing and had that wonderful glow that pregnant women had. The kind that made people smile. Especially parents. Babies were all that was right in the world. Fresh, innocent, sweet-smelling, and giggly.

Then they turned into teens. And their fathers became the stupidest people ever born in the history of ever. Funny how his daughter's latest jibe ricocheted around his mind. The boy was less of a pain but needed more eyes on where he was going and what he was up to. He suspected his oldest had been taking his truck out after Jon had gone to bed. Ben needed watching.

"Technically, I'm no longer Mrs. Warden, but I kept his name." She blushed like a girl and waved a hand in front of her face. "Darn hormones," she muttered. "Please call me Trix," she smiled again and lit the barn with it. "I would change my last name, but I sell my paintings as T. Warden, so I'm stuck with it." She licked her lower lip, looking flush and lovely.

"Trix, it is," he said, cutting through her mountain of words. She'd given him a lot of information to process at once, but he followed it and came to the most salient facts. She was single. And pregnant. And a starving artist.

As such, it made no sense that he was here to talk to *her* about renovating the barn. He turned his attention to the couple.

Trix waved a hand toward the others. "This is my cousin Brenna and her husband Jett Somers."

Jett was the first to speak. "You're the guy who built this?"

"And you're the guy who helped Billie and her mom, Juliet last summer. You made a big difference in their lives."

Jett nodded. "I am that guy, but today I'm here to observe, not buy."

Somers looked all business and higher end than the people Jon usually worked with. More New York than New England. Figured, since he was a wildly successful venture capitalist. He'd put money and his connections to work to help Billie Adamson change the world. Dickens had buzzed for months about it; a sickly teenage girl and her single mom had their lives changed completely. Couldn't have happened to a more deserving family.

In his peripheral vision, Trix pursed her lips and tossed her cousin a look. Brenna squeezed her husband's hand.

"I'm the one interested in buying the barn, Mr. Carpenter," Trix said clearly.

"Jon," he said with a smile as he turned toward her. "Just Jon."

She nodded and stepped closer. Her eyes were a green hazel and assessed him.

"What can I help you with?" he asked, hiding his surprise. Her husband was gone. Maybe she wasn't such a starving artist after all. All his assumptions flew out of his head, and he looked at her with fresh eyes. Still pretty, still pregnant. Not broke but interested in scooping up a bargain for overdue taxes. Maybe she had a load of cash from her divorce settlement.

"Since this building is going for taxes and people can't usually tour ahead of time, I played the baby card at the town hall,"—she waved a hand over her baby bump— "and they were kind enough to give me one hour inside the barn to decide if it suits my needs. Since you know this building intimately, we'll walk through it while I explain what I need done."

"It's a horse barn," he said. "Basically a stable for horses. That isn't what you're looking for?" She'd been lucky to get this time inside. Stan must have had taken pity on the pregnant lady. The town administrator had a soft spot for ladies in need. That, and the auction was tomorrow, so the town office had been extra kind.

"It'll be much more than a horse barn to me," she responded with a breathy excitement that caught at his lips and lifted the corners. His revised assessment appeared accurate. She had money. How she came to have it wasn't his concern. His smile grew.

He couldn't help it. There was something about Trix Warden that made him happy inside. The feeling was foreign and from long ago. It took a moment to recognize it.

"Show me," he said.

Chapter Two

When Trix announced she was the one buying, Jon Carpenter heard her. He *listened*. How refreshing. He'd given her a nod and accepted that the short, very round, baby vessel deserved his focus.

Smart man. She liked smart men.

Good looking, too, if you liked men in shearling jackets, blue jeans, and well-worn work boots. His eyes were dark brown and broody, ringed with thick black lashes. He looked mid-thirties and capable. His pepper dark hair held strands of silver and his eyes had squinted too much in the sunshine or the man liked to laugh. Either way, he wore his crow's feet well.

A vestige of womanhood woke and stretched inside her. She gave him her best smile and stepped closer.

He'd asked to be shown what she wanted done. She hoped her plans were manageable and not too grand for a building that was, for all intents and purposes, a stable.

"Thanks, I have a dream for this place," she said, with a gesture encompassing the floor to ceiling and from front to back. "If anything I ask for is out of line or out of budget, speak up." She'd wait to give him her deadline. No point scaring the man off.

"I have no problem speaking my mind. Whether you hear me or not is another story." He deadpanned.

She tilted her head, surprised. "Are you teasing me, Jon?" *Smart and funny. Bonus.*

"Perfect," he said with a sly smile. "It's as if you can read my mind. But clients who don't like what they hear often use selective hearing. You should know I mean what I say." All business now, he pulled a notebook out of his inside jacket pocket and a pen out from behind his ear. "Give me the details. I'll tell you if you miss anything."

She liked a plain-spoken person. Dale had never been straightforward. He'd agree to things then whine when it was time to move ahead. Making dinner reservations had become a battle. He'd say her choice was fine, but at the restaurant he'd whine about the food, the table, the price, and sometimes her company. He often wanted to have other people with them to avoid talking with her. It had taken his leaving for her to see it. She'd been blind.

But Jon wasn't Dale and Jon heard what she had to say. She blinked and cleared Dale out of her head.

She was talking to Jon Carpenter now and that changed everything. Confidence in the contractor blossomed and she gave him a brisk nod. "Thank you. I'll listen," she promised.

Mutual respect established she pushed on.

She walked to stand at his side. "I plan to have a gallery of stalls for potters, weavers, and other kinds of artists." She raised her hands to toward the high ceiling. She loved that there was a loft. It provided more floor space she'd need.

"My paintings will hang from the rafters down the center of the barn." She envisioned her works hanging above shoppers' heads. "I hope people will be looking up all the time. Looking up and smiling."

He covered a smile with his question. "You're a painter and the other artists will work in different mediums."

"That's right. Crafters and artisans."

"Okay. And you want the other artists to be in these narrow stalls?"

"Can you combine stalls so they're twice as big as now?" A couple of people had asked for workspace as well as display.

"Sure. If you need three turned into one, I can do that, too. But moving beams will be expensive."

"Okay, then we won't move beams, just the separations between the stalls." A flush of warmth overtook her. She couldn't be sure if it was hormonal or just that Jon seemed to get what she needed. This might be easier than she thought. "Also, I'd like an office with room for the baby. Could you build one in the loft?"

"I could. I'll do a staircase with a landing. That way, it's not a straight shot down. Safer for you both."

The warmth stole into her cheeks at his caring. "How kind to think of that."

"It's nothing," he responded, deflecting her gratitude. "If you want the barn to be warm enough for people, you'll need insulation and drywall. I could hide wiring more easily that way, too. There are building codes I have to follow." He said the last firmly, as if expecting an argument. "And you'll need a heating system."

She spun and looked at the walls. "Of course. I wanted the barn look for the exterior walls, but I see why you'd suggest otherwise. It makes sense." She adjusted her vision, accepting his advice. New England had cold winters and insulation and heat would be important. She mentally added to the budget and cringed inside.

"I suggest a heat pump. In summer, it'll act as an air conditioner."

"In a building this large?" Jett asked.

"I'll install ceiling fans, there, there and there," he said, indicating the placement. "In winter the warm air will be kept down where the public is, but in summer with the fans' direction reversed the cool air will rise. If you need extra heat in your office, I can install a safe electric baseboard heater."

"In spring and fall, the fans may be all the air flow needed."

"Right," he said with a grin that seemed for her alone. Another thrill shot through her at Jon's intent focus. She told herself the focus was for the job, not her, but that tiny piece of woman inside her argued the point.

"Don't want to lie. The drywall and wiring will add time to the project. And time is money. What budget am I working with?"

She named a price. When a serious frown settled on Jon's face, she had a twinge of doubt. What could she scale back?

Jett shifted beside her. Brenna looked at her husband. "Spill it," she murmured.

Jett leaned into Trix's ear and whispered. "I want to invest, and that budget won't cut it. Triple it."

"Jett! I can't do that. It'll take forever to repay you." Shocked by his offer, Trix blanched. Jon nodded and gave Jett a speculative glance.

The contractor cleared his throat. "I agree. The budget's too low for what you have in mind. Maybe if you were only open in the warm months?"

"No, this is year-round. It has to be."

"Then I can't do the job the way you need it done, not for that budget." He shook his head and his gaze looked regretful. "I understand what you want, and I can get back to you with an estimate if you decide to take your cousin's help. Otherwise, I'm out."

She looked at the glorious space. "There's nowhere else in town. Nothing that will give me the room I need for the vision I have." She frowned. But she hadn't come this far to turn back now. "I'll work out something with Jett and call you."

She needed to be here in Dickens to raise this baby. She needed regular work hours and a place where the baby could be with her while she worked on this side of her business. She had a plan that *had to* work.

Jon tipped two fingers to his forehead in a salute and strode toward the door. "I'll wait for your call," he said before he opened the door and stepped outside. The warmth she'd felt earlier deserted her at his exit. She shivered as she felt the still cold inside the barn.

"That went well," she said. Except she hadn't told him all this work had to be done by December first. Inside, she groaned. The rush job would likely cost more. She cast Jett a sidelong glance only to see him grinning like a mad clown. "What?"

"I'll quadruple the loan," he said with a smirk.

"And I'll help with anything else you need," Brenna stated in a no-nonsense voice. "Starting with all your social media and website. Whatever marketing you need, I'll do." Her cousin worked with Jett using her marketing experience on the Research and Development company he'd invested in with Billie Adamson. She was all of fourteen now and from what Jett said, poised to change the world. Her discovery would extend battery life by double.

"Thanks, I'm grateful, but I have to talk to him again."

She waved her thanks as she dashed for the door to catch up to Jon. She dreaded his reaction when she gave him the deadline. But the man had the decency to listen to her, so he needed to hear everything.

Jon was about to put his truck into reverse when a flash of movement caught his eye. Trix Warden sprinted toward him, the ends of her pumpkin-colored scarf flying as she moved too quickly. He lowered the passenger side window as she put two hands up to wave. She did a half skid to a stop and grasped the door.

"What are you doing running around on wet leaves? They're slippery." He didn't care that he sounded gruff; she'd scared him half to death.

She squinted against the bright sun and then to look at the bare ground. Her face when she turned it back to meet his gaze looked curious. But she didn't point out the obvious. There were no wet leaves anywhere. They hadn't had rain in a week. "Sometimes," she said breathlessly, "I get too excited to remember I'm not as nimble as I was a few months ago."

"You scared the hell out of me," he admitted with a shake of his head. "My wife had a fall with our son, and it was a rough few hours until we learned the baby was okay. Don't let me see you forget again." His voice was rougher than intended. "Sorry, flashback I guess."

It had been a rainy day and the leaves had been slick. Melody had fallen hard. Her face, pale and scared, filled his vision.

Trix Warden nodded. "Are they okay now?" she asked. "Your wife and son?"

"He is, if you count being a sixteen-year-old butthead okay." He said it with humor, but there was truth in it, too. "My wife passed away a couple of years ago." He hesitated. "Not from the fall." He squinted at her, at the memories of his life with Melody.

"I'm sorry," Trix murmured, gaze soft in sympathy. He didn't want to see her soft side. It pulled at him, made him want something he'd set aside, didn't have time for, and didn't want.

He hit the unlock button for her door. "Climb in if you want to add something to the discussion about the job." There was a nip in the air and fall in New England could bring an early, freak snowfall. It was only Hallowe'en, but he'd seen it before. Sure there was sun right now, but heavy clouds could appear quickly. He hoped Trix Warden could stick to talking about the job and keep things impersonal.

He'd be safe that way and wouldn't have to think about how she made him feel.

"Thanks, yes." She opened the passenger door and climbed in. When she hit the power button for the window, she closed them inside the warming interior of the pickup. Needing space, he settled his back against his door. He waited, enjoying the view of her pretty eyes and upturned nose. Up close like this he noticed a few light freckles across her nose. Trix Warden was one pretty woman.

"No surprise, but I can't do this without Jett's help. It was kind of him to offer. I didn't expect to find such a perfect building. But the remodel will take more than I have budgeted." She smiled and smoothed her tummy. "I need to live in Dickens with the baby. I'm on my own and my mom and grandmother are here. Not to mention my cousins and I are close. I planned to ask Brenna's advice on marketing, but to have her offer to do all the work blows my mind."

He nodded, glad she had a good family to back her, both with the business and the baby. "I figured you planned to live here. If we work this out, I'll make sure you have the room you need for the baby." This woman seemed unstoppable. She was single and pregnant but instead of shrinking from her situation, she faced it head on. Blunt about her plans, her needs and honest in her negotiations, with Trix Warden, what you saw is what you got. He liked that about her already. "You'll have all you need. I promise."

Her smile lit the cab of his truck. "The other thing is, I need this work done pronto. I've promised the artists that they'll have a good Christmas season." She flushed red but held his gaze as if searching for the truth. "I try to keep my word. Promises are important things. I don't give mine lightly."

He held up both hands. "You want this done before the Christmas sales kick in?" She should've come to him in July, but he'd hear her out before saying so.

"It's a big ask. If I'd found the right building sooner"—she waved the thought away— "I need to open on Black Friday." She bit her lower lip at her outrageous request. "December first at the latest."

The day after Thanksgiving kicked off a frenzy of holiday shopping. "I get that. But you must realize people leave Dickens in a flood for the big box stores to get their holiday bargains."

"I'm not offering bargains. I'm offering art. Some fine, some more craft than strictly art. But nothing will be cheap."

The idea sounded ludicrous. "No one comes to a barn in a New England town to buy fine art and expensive hobby stuff."

She gasped, raised her eyebrows and he wanted, more than anything, to take the words back. But Trix Warden deserved the courtesy of hearing the truth. He let his comment lie between them, watching her closely.

If she cried, he wasn't sure how to respond.

Chapter Three

If Jon had learned anything as a contractor, it was not to comment on a client's business plan. The proof that he'd poked the bear showed in Trix's pinched lips. Deriding her dream had been wrong and he badly wanted to backpedal. Before he could pull up the right words, she began talking.

Her eyes cool and watchful, she said, "I've been in touch with some of the best artisans in New England." She was pretty when she got haughty and tried to quell her temper.

"I'm sure you have." He nodded. "Forget I said anything. You know your business better than I do."

She ignored him. "They'll bring their clientele and I'll do a ton of marketing. I have several paintings in a Manhattan gallery, but our exclusive agreement ends at the New York state line."

Yes, and there it was, the expression of her success. Her paintings hung in fancy galleries for rich people. An internet search would tell him about her work and career in ten seconds.

"You're the big draw."

"I am. I'm not a household name, but I'm getting a lot of attention." Her gaze held his steady and purposeful.

"And you need to strike while the iron's hot."

She nodded. "In a couple of years, there'll be a new artist that'll be the new hot thing. By then, I want a steady income from this market. I want this barn to be a destination. Dickens is already a draw over the holidays, but my plan is to bring people all year long."

She had smarts and determination. And kept her promises when she could. And she'd promised these artisans that they'd have a place to show their work.

"I was wrong," he said. "If anyone can do this, you can." After her speech, he believed. And he'd do what he could to help her.

She shrugged; a woman determined to get what she wanted. He admired her grit.

"I don't have a choice. I must keep my options open and provide for this baby. Which, by the way is a total miracle." She smiled in maternal joy, and he remembered the same expression on Melody.

"The gallery owner understood that I couldn't depend on her support alone," Trix continued. "After her shock wore off, Cecilia offered to tell select clients about my plans and where to find me. In return she requested I call it something other than a gallery. I came up with market." She sniffed. "But market suits the small-town New England vibe. And especially a renovated barn."

He slid a hand down his face. "I guess the hot new things in the art world don't leave for the backwoods of New England."

"Not often. Unless they're already there, of course. But I live in Brooklyn, and she expected me to be close at hand."

He nodded; glad she'd returned to Dickens. "Market seems like the right word. Could you call it a studio? Would the gallery owner object to that? Studio might sound more artsy to clients who care about that stuff."

"That's an idea," she allowed with a nod. "I owe Cecilia for giving me a leg up when I needed it. In fairness, I chose not to call it a gallery. She's still showing my work and making me money." She smiled. "All I want is to live my life here, near family, and take care of my baby at the same time." She smoothed her hand over her baby bump in a protective sweep. "I'll see what my marketing expert cousin thinks of calling it a studio."

He'd seen his wife brush a hand over her belly a million times. Still made him smile.

He was glad something did.

"I've got to get home," he said with a tinge of regret. He'd enjoyed the conversation, the peek into someone else's life. A person new to him was rare in Dickens. "It's Hallowe'en and I have decorating to do at the house, or my daughter will kill me. They're expecting it done when they get home from school."

"So you have a son and a daughter." Sympathy rose in her gaze again as she realized his kids had lost their mom. He looked away from it as his jaw tightened.

"My kids, AKA teens from hell. A boy, sixteen, and my girl, fifteen." He shook his head and chuckled. "I'm thirty-five, and yes, we had them young, but they're the best thing I've ever done. As soon as the aliens return my real kids to me, we'll be fine. Meantime, I'm tearing my hair out. Ben is determined to be a man before his time and Blair is defiant with a capital D."

"You were a kid yourself," Trix said, her tone shocked as she did the math. Thirty-five minus sixteen equaled real young. "Twice."

"What I said about Ben wanting to be a man and Blair being defiant? Melody used to say we had one for each of us. She got it right. I was Ben and she was Blair back then. Ben was born when we were married six months."

She didn't even raise an eyebrow. "But you made it work. You were happy."

"Yes, we were. We didn't get to go to college or do any of the things our friends were doing. Instead, I joined my dad in carpentry, learned a lot about other building trades and here we are." No college, no degrees, but he'd built a good life for his family. "Melody was taking night classes when she was diagnosed. She'd have made a good nurse."

"I'm sorry for your loss. But like you said, here we are." Trix sighed in sympathy. He'd been left with a lot of responsibility when his wife had passed. But he'd shouldered a lot as a young father, and he'd had years of experience before he had to go it alone.

"I'm thirty-seven and considered a geriatric pregnancy. Thirty-seven doesn't seem old, but that word makes me feel ancient." She wondered if the doctor had used it to scare her into taking care of herself, not that she needed the extra push. From the get-go she'd been extra cautious. She let the thought drift away. "None of us hits our mid-thirties without some baggage."

He nodded. "Agreed. And, for the record, I don't agree that you're geriatric." He winced at the word which made her grin.

"You're very kind." And thoughtful, but she kept that to herself. This wasn't anything but a business negotiation and tossing compliments at the man was out of place. One, fine, but two? Overkill and a bit desperate if she were brutally honest.

She spoke again. "I guess I'll see whether the aliens replace this little one in a few years." But she couldn't imagine having a teen, much less one that drove her to tearing out hair. "I wasn't rebellious in my teens. I waited until I went to college and then married a man my mom didn't like much." She sighed. Actually, no one in the family took to Dale. "Long story."

Jon nodded. "What about the baby's dad? He's not around?"

He would naturally assume the father wasn't her ex; most people would. "Boring story." She set her lips, so he'd see the subject was off limits. She couldn't get into it. Ever again. She'd explained it all to the people she loved and that was all she had to say.

When she didn't elaborate, he went on. "Enjoy the fun years while they last. Just this morning I was called the stupidest person ever born in the history of ever."

She eased her lips to make room for a smile. She was sure he planned it that way. "Ouch. What for?"

"I asked her why she didn't want waffles anymore. What's wrong with offering waffles for breakfast? It was a simple question." Bewilderment filled his gaze.

"Yes, it does *seem* simple, but she's fifteen. I doubt anything is simple for her right now." She was straining her knowledge of teens while trying to recall some of her emotions from that time. Mood swings, she remembered those. "Is there anything else going on with her?"

He sighed, long and gustily. "I'm not sure. One day she's happy like she used to be, and I think I imagine all the other times she's a stranger."

"I lost my dad young. I don't remember him much. Just flashes. But when I hit my teens, I missed him a lot. Not him, the man, but the idea of having a dad. A man to pick me up in his truck like the other girls had. A man to cheer at my high school volleyball games." Old memories and loneliness filled her mind. She darted a glance at him. "The other girls had them. Dads, stepdads, heck, even their mom's boyfriends showed up at the gym."

When Laurel had been dating the mayor, he'd offered to pick up Trix from school sometimes, but her mom had refused his help. She'd been stubborn about keeping her dating life separate from her home life. It wasn't a bad thing to do, but Trix didn't want to do the same. No, if a good man showed up in her life, then she'd take a chance. She'd be dating by now if she hadn't got pregnant. There was no time to date when she needed to make a living for two.

She frowned. She'd never considered that maybe her mom's choices back then had had consequences for both of them. Unseen and unknowable consequences that Trix didn't want to repeat.

Jon nodded, oddly touched by Trix's explanation of her teens. Blair missed her mother. He understood on the surface, but he hadn't considered how many reminders she lived with every day. Poor kid. "I wish she'd talk about her mom, but she doesn't. I suspect she's afraid to cry in front of me." A prickle built in his eyes, and he blinked to clear them. "The waffles I offered were frozen. Her mom made homemade."

Trix reached out toward his hand where it lay on his thigh, but she pulled back before touching him. Too bad, he could use a comforting pat. But the warmth in her gaze did the job anyway. "I can give you a recipe if you need it. Or maybe try to recall if she used a mix."

"Blair would remember. She spent time in the kitchen with Melody."

"Then maybe she'd like to make the waffles? Fifteen's not too young to cook."

He resisted the idea. "I didn't want to put that on her. I'm their father. It's my job to feed them, do the laundry, and clean up after them." Wasn't it? That's what Melody had said. What she'd asked him to do. She'd wanted him to be there for their kids, to take care of their needs.

Trix pinched her lips together. Clearly, she had an opinion.

"Spill it. I can see you've got something to say."

She shook her head. "What do I know about teenagers? It's been twenty years since I was their age. What I need is your promise to have my studio ready in time for Black Friday."

Back to business. It was for the best. This woman was a client, nothing more.

He consulted his scheduler on his phone, but since he'd already promised to work if the budget was increased, all he had to do was move up the timeline.

"I can get it done. It'll be close, but doable." Especially if he recruited Ben to help. It was time the boy started to learn the business. Even if he never took over, his son should learn his way around a toolbox and power tools. "There may be leftover finishing touches. You need to know that."

THE RUMBALL RUMBA: A DICKENS HOLIDAY

"How soon can I have your estimate?"

"I'll have it for you by tomorrow noon."

"Good. Maybe we can meet at Dorrit's Diner. My mom works there. She'll give us the quietest booth in the back."

"Laurel's your mom?" He should've seen the resemblance, but with Trix's coloring being different from her mom's, he'd missed it. Their features were similar though.

"Yes, and my grandmother owns Tiny Tim's Dance Studio."

"Sure," he said. "I know the place. Blair and Ben took lessons there. She tried ballet but after a week, she said she hated being told what to do. Ben took to tap. He liked it and continued for a couple of years. Until his friends razzed him."

"Of course," she said with a smile. "Lots of people used to dance as children. But something happens and they lose the fun, or the thrill or sports take over."

"I guess." But he frowned because Ben had loved it so much. Melody had gotten sick, and Ben had quit. "I need to get home. My house won't decorate itself. Spooky takes time." He wanted to get away from this woman who made him think too much.

Tomorrow, at Dorrit's, he wouldn't let the conversation veer into the personal. No, he'd keep it strictly business. With any luck he'd only see her on the job site when she came by to inspect it. "You're going back to New York soon?"

"No. I live at my grandmother's for now. I moved in last week after being here most weekends through the summer. When I say there was nothing else in town that would suit my plans, I meant it. I've been looking for what seems like ages. Gram's got lots of room and I want to be at the barn all the way through the renovations."

He hated when clients said that. They asked too many questions and sucked time away from the work. And then, inevitably, they complained when he fell behind. He'd tell her his ground rules tomorrow at Dorrit's.

Right now, he was needed on his front lawn where he planned to set up a graveyard with skeletons climbing out of the ground.

Chapter Four

November 1-Auction Day

Bright and early the next morning, Jon tapped on Blair's bedroom door. Her usual groan and shriek came from the other side of the door. He shook his head. She slept heavily and often didn't wake up when her alarm went off. That's why she'd taken to shrieking when she saw the time.

Apparently, being fifteen meant she had a lot more to do to get ready in the morning. Her hair, makeup, and anything else she deemed important took more time than she gave herself. She was a natural beauty, if only she'd believe it. But no, she had to dye her hair pink, shave half of it off and wear black lipstick. The lipstick color was new, and he hoped it went away as suddenly as it had come.

"You could go to bed earlier," he suggested for the twentieth time. "Or leave your phone in the kitchen overnight," he muttered more to himself than to her.

"AAHH. Stop talking!"

"Okay. But I thought you'd like to make waffles from scratch this morning."

The door opened a crack. One eye, ringed in yesterday's black goo, glared at him. "You mean like Mom made?"

"Since you hate my freezer waffles."

She blinked and stifled a yawn. "Do I have time?"

"I'll drive you to school, so you don't have to walk." She rarely allowed him to drive her. He was far too weird— Goofy? Whatever— for her to be seen with him on most days.

"What's going on? If she gets a ride, I do, too." Ben was already dressed and walking toward the bathroom down the hall.

"I've got the bowl out and the mix she used," he directed at Blair. He paused, waiting while she considered.

"Did you get an egg out of the fridge? She used an egg."

He held up two fingers. "Recipe calls for two if we make a double batch." Melody had used a whole grain waffle mix. Something he'd learned by digging into the farthest reaches of the pantry. The mix he'd found last night was too old to use. He'd raced to the grocery store after dinner and left Ben to hand out the candy to the kids. There were fewer with each passing year. The neighborhood had matured, the kids grown. "If we make double there'll be some for breakfast tomorrow, too."

"Okay!" Blair squealed like an excited five-year-old and disappeared back into her room, presumably to dress.

His daughter's smile had made his heart thud. He'd missed it and couldn't recall when he'd seen it last. "Good, I'll see you downstairs," he said to the closed door.

Ben had already barreled down. "There won't be any left," he announced. "I'm starved."

That boy was always starved. Jon chuckled as he followed his son. He'd been the same at Ben's age. Half the time he had his head stuck in the fridge, rummaging. The other half he'd been chasing girls.

He frowned and thought of Trix Warden, facing motherhood alone. At least she wasn't a teenager, which made him think of girls his son might be chasing. "Ben, we need to talk."

He checked up the staircase, but Blair was still in her room. He walked into the kitchen to find Ben chowing down on a leftover piece of pizza. He wasn't sure how old it was. But the kid had a cast iron stomach, so he let it go. He tossed the empty delivery box into the recycle bin because Ben wouldn't.

"What?" Ben asked when he saw his father's expression.

"Are you seeing any girls?"

Color slashed across his cheeks, but his gaze shifted to the wall behind his father. He crammed the last of the pizza slice into his mouth to avoid speaking.

"So, are you seeing girls or one in particular?" Jon pressed.

"Maybe." The word came out garbled, but it was clear enough.

Jon nodded. "You'll find condoms in the bathroom cabinet tonight. I won't be checking, but if you run out, put them on the grocery list."

"Dad!!"

"I'm serious, Ben. You know I was nineteen and happy you came along. But don't limit your choices in life until you're sure where life's going to take you."

Ben narrowed his gaze but nodded once. "I get it."

Melody would've been better at this, but he believed his son understood.

Blair might need a bit more finesse and he hoped he had time to find the right words. She was only fifteen, but lots of girls her age got caught. By love. By the heat of the moment. By their own innocence. By boys who thought nothing of taking advantage...

His stomach dropped to his toes and eating waffles flew out the window.

"And one more thing," he said to his half-grown man. "You never, *ever*, take advantage of a girl who's been drinking, or doing drugs. You never, *ever*, take what isn't offered and you *always* get a yes before you kiss her for the first time."

"Dad! I'm not a moron."

"Of course not, but there'll come a time when this head,"—he tapped his temple— "quits being in charge. You get me?"

"Yes. I get it." He sounded sullen, and embarrassed, but Jon was glad he'd spoken up and that Ben had stayed in the room to hear it.

Too antsy to sit in chairs, Trix stood beside Brenna and Jett and watched the large screen inside the town hall's meeting room. The County was holding their annual real estate auction and three properties were on the block. Auctions were live streamed which meant there could be bidders from anywhere. A slow thudding in her chest proved how nervous she felt.

"This should be over quickly," she muttered to her cousin. She nodded to Stan, the town clerk, who'd been kind enough to let her inside the barn yesterday. Stan was past retirement age and gave her a thumbs up.

Brenna nodded. "This is fun." Beside Brenna, Jett shifted, looking like a panther on the prowl. He was here to win and Trix felt infinitely grateful this man was on her side.

On the screen, a house from a neighboring town sold after a short, pitched battle between two brothers, each outbidding the other in rapid succession. They'd gone to the County seat in person and Trix decided they'd driven in separate vehicles. After a couple of nerve-wracking minutes the gavel came down for the final time and the brother wearing a denim jacket won the bidding. The other looked like he wanted to punch him.

Brenna leaned in. "They're twins. Maybe they've always fought over who gets what."

The next house came up with four people bidding. Two were remote and bid by phone while a man dressed in sport coat and slacks that screamed real estate agent bid higher. It looked like the man would win the auction. But suddenly a fifth bid came in from a woman who stood to the side. She made a much higher offer that crushed her opponents. When sport coat guy conceded, the woman shed happy tears.

Trix spoke. "She must love the house. It means something more to her than an address."

Next, the Scott barn was announced. Her barn. The lot number, and the legal address in Dickens scrolled across the bottom of the screen and Trix held her breath as the auctioneer began. Her belly clenched as she hoped the two remote bidders had lost interest.

No such luck.

"There's a bid," Trix breathed, devastated. She tapped her phone to indicate her new bid. The other party bid again. She firmed her lips and glanced at Jett, who nodded back.

"End it," he said. "Like the bidder did with the last house. Add ten grand."

She upped her bid by five thousand dollars. And apparently, that was more than the other party thought the barn was worth. The bidding ended and the gavel came down on the block.

She'd won the auction and a kind of eerie calm overcame her. She sank into the chair immediately behind her, glad for the support.

"Right," she said, "now things get hairy." She drew in several calming breaths. Her to-do list exploded behind her eyes, making her a tad dizzy. Either that or she was hyperventilating. She wished Jon were here. She'd feel more at ease if she could see his calm, reassuring face.

"Great job, you got it without using your highest bid. Now you can put that extra five grand into renovations." Jett smiled widely and shook Trix's hand.

"Time to call Jon and confirm your lunch date with him," Brenna said with a sly smirk.

"You mean our business meeting," she corrected Brenna. Sure, they'd shared some personal conversation yesterday in his truck, but it didn't mean anything more than idle chatter. From what she'd gathered parents of teens complained about them all the time. No biggie that he'd shared some stuff with her. He probably wouldn't do it again.

Despite deciding to keep the discussion all business, the moment Jon slid into the back booth at Dorrit's Diner and looked into Trix's happy green hazel gaze, he started with, "Thanks for the advice on the waffles. It worked."

She beamed at him. "That's great. I'm glad." She had her laptop on the table, closed. "How were they? As good as Blair remembered?"

"Absolutely. Ben pitched in by setting the table and warming the syrup in the microwave, the way Melody used to." He couldn't wipe the grin off his face.

"It sounds lovely, like a real family breakfast." She tilted her head, looking pleased for him. For them all.

"Not to brag, but I cooked sausages." Ridiculous the way he soaked up her approval. As if what a client thought of his parenting skills mattered. *Give your head a shake.*

"That's not a brag, not at all," she teased. She rolled her shoulders to indicate pride in herself. "And I'm not taking credit."

He laughed out loud. It had been years since he'd felt release like this.

Laurel appeared at their table, order pad in hand, her eyes alight and looking from one to the other of them.

Trix pulled her laptop over to sit in front of her. "Hi, Mom." She lifted the lid and raised her eyebrows as if her mom was intruding.

Jon looked at Laurel. "I haven't seen you with an order pad in forever."

"Good afternoon to you, too, Jon. What'll you have?" She asked cheerily.

"Lunch."

"With my daughter?"

"Yes?"

"To what purpose?"

"Oh, for pity's sake, Mom. We're here to discuss the estimate on the barn if you must know." She narrowed her eyes at Laurel. "And I told you that when I came in and asked for *this* booth. Not everyone in Dickens needs to listen in on my business."

Laurel pouted. "Okay, it's just that you both looked..."

Trix glared as her mom's words trailed away suggestively. "What? We both looked what?"

"Happy, is all. Just happy." She cleared her throat. "I know what Jon wants, but what'll you have sweetie?"

"Soup of the day and a grilled ham and cheese."

"Good choice," Trix's mother said with a smile and strode away.

"She didn't need her order pad after all."

"Like you said, she hasn't needed one in years. She knows what all the locals like. She also knows I love the butternut squash soup, so that was a given."

"I should've ordered something different to mess with her." He winked.

"Next time," Trix said with an evil grin.

Jon wasn't sure there'd be a next time, because from here on they could meet at the barn as he worked. She'd said she wanted to be there throughout the renos. He didn't like the idea because clients didn't often understand the process involved in the job. It was a waste of time to have to explain every step. Usually, he charged more because of the aggravation.

"When do you get possession?"

"Very soon, but I sweet-talked Stan, the town clerk, into giving me the keys early. We can start as soon as possible."

"Of course you sweet-talked him. Stan's a sucker for a sob story and a pretty woman. But I'd hate to see him lose his job." Sure, Stan was looking to retire, but still, his pension could be at stake.

Trix shook her head. "The mayor and the town administrator agreed to turn a blind eye to Stan helping me out. I went to kindergarten with the administrator. Half the town council comes here for lunch. And the others are friendly with my grandmother. They're happy I'm moving back and plan to bring a business to town that encourages tourism."

He nodded. "One of the advantages of small-town life. Everyone knows everyone."

She laughed. "A doubled-edged sword sometimes. I can't tell you how much speculation there is about the baby's father. There are a thousand theories and not a one of them makes me look good."

"Despite their curiosity, they want to help." He could imagine the scenarios people would dream up about her.

Her gaze roved his face as if looking for something familiar. "Did we know each other when we were kids here?"

Jon shook his head. "Dad and I moved here for a job when I first got married. We liked Dickens so we stayed. After Mom died, Dad retired, moved to Florida and rather than move with him, I decided to carry on with the business." That decision had proven a good one. He'd been able to provide for his growing family, make good friends and the servers in the local restaurants remembered his favorite meals.

Life was good. His dad was happy doing odd jobs for the retirees where he lived, and he and his wife visited every summer to avoid the heat.

And he liked that he lived in a town that was run by people who cared about helping citizens achieve their goals.

"I need to tell you that you have a good reputation down at the town hall," she said. "I doubt that they'd have helped me out except that I said you'd be doing the work."

"Whoa, there. You haven't heard my estimate yet."

She laughed; a low sexy chuckle that turned his insides warm. He sat back. This would go nowhere. She was pregnant and in no way, shape, or form, ready to get into a thing with him. Friendly business relations, though, that was something they could manage.

With that thought front and center, he reached into his jacket pocket and slid a printed estimate across the table for her to read.

A full five minutes later, after she checked her laptop several times, took notes and sighed over the figures, she looked up.

"Okay, we can do this, but are you sure you can stick to the timeline?"

"Since I'm the guy who built the barn, I'd say there will be no nasty surprises to upset the budget or the timeline."

"Cute." She offered him her hand across the table. He took it and they shook. Her hand was soft, warm and her shake was firm. The handshake of a person who knew what they were after and would get it.

Laurel arrived with a tray at her shoulder, their meals balanced expertly. His burger and salad looked delicious, as Laurel set it in front of him. He said a silent thank you to Melody for encouraging him to eat more greens.

"Nice to see a man eat something other than fries," Trix quipped. "My ex was determined to clog every artery he could."

"Melody kept her eye on our diets. She told me when we were old that I'd thank her." He used his fork on the salad and enjoyed the crunch of crisp lettuce and greens. When he glanced up, he paused. He needed to quit talking about things that made Trix well up with tears.

"Sorry, I don't mean to remind you of my loss. Most of the time, I'm happy to have the memory come to me. It's all right." He set down his fork, prepared to let the food wait.

Trix waved her hand in front of her face as she collected herself. Then she gave him a faded smile. "Half the time, my leaky eyes are just hormones. I hope." Her smile brightened. "A fine pair we are."

"I bet your sense of humor got you through a lot of that baggage you mentioned."

"As a matter of fact, it did." She grinned. "Now, who's footing the bill for lunch?"

Chapter Five

"You'd think by my age my mother would butt out of my life." Trix's complaint was the third in ten minutes. She and Brenna were in their grandmother's dining room, looking over the options Brenna had come up with for the website.

Brenna chuckled. "You're thirty-seven and pregnant without a husband. Of course she'll look at every available man within a five-hundred-mile radius. Be grateful she hasn't placed ads. 'Good man wanted by successful artist entrepreneur' could work."

"Funny. How did I land in a family full of comedians? You should take that on the road."

"Drink your tea and make a decision."

"Fine. This one. I like the colors and the flow of the site. I like that the request to sign up for the newsletter is on the side rather than a huge pop-up mid-screen."

"You told me often enough that the site should be about the art, not the newsletter." Brenna sighed. "Let's see how many people sign up and look at it again in six months."

"Okay by me." Trix sipped her peppermint tea and sat back, rubbing her bump. She wasn't sure if she comforted the baby nestled inside or herself more. But she loved the round firmness. "I need to get more clothes. The pants I have are getting snug."

"Wear dresses. They're more in style now anyway."

"Something clingy like models and actresses wear?"

"Sure, why not? You have a great figure and you're beautifully proportioned."

Her cheeks warmed at the praise. "That's not how I feel but I'll take your word for it."

"Not just my word," Brenna said slyly. "I noticed that the contractor checked you out pretty thoroughly. And then as he closed the door of the barn, he looked again."

"He was probably making sure the door didn't stick. How would it look if the builder couldn't shut the door?"

"Right," Brenna drawled.

"Hmph. And he was only focused on me because he wanted the work." She shook her head. "Hey, did you say anything about this so-called check-out to my mother? Is that why she was nosy at lunch?"

Next time she and Jon went anywhere it wouldn't be Dorrit's. "I'm sure he only sees me as his client because he let me handle the bill. He said if he paid it, he'd just add it to the budget." He'd been joking, but Brenna and her nosy family needn't know how they made each other laugh.

It was good to keep a friendly attitude with your contractor. When the inevitable hiccups in the job came along, she'd have a better idea of how to read the man. That was the only reason she thought of him again and again. She wanted to get a handle on the man, nothing more.

"Maybe a dress or two is a good idea. I can wear them immediately after the baby comes, too. I could look for a Christmas red one." With sparkles to keep the season cheery. She loved sparkles.

"And silver," Brenna said with a nod. "That would be great."

"Hello!" Gram's voice sounded from the front hall. "Brenna," she said with a smile in her voice. "Are you here to help with the website?"

"Decision's made on that already, Gram," Brenna assured her. She rose and hugged the new arrival.

"Trix, stay in your seat," her Gram tutted and kissed the top of her head in greeting. "How are you today? You look rosy and happy."

"I feel great. I've had a productive day." At least five items ticked off her to-do list. "Thanks to Brenna and her crackerjack skills." She opened her mouth to say more, but Gram lifted a hand and waved her to silence.

"I've already heard that you won the auction, had lunch with a handsome man, and now, you've decided on your website. You're a powerhouse." She touched Trix's cheek and the love in her eyes warmed her.

"Thanks, Gram."

"But don't overdo."

"I'm being careful. I have a canvas I need help moving. Brenna's helping."

"First I've heard of it," her cousin muttered with a dose of humor. "How was your day at the dance studio, Gram?" she asked.

"Wonderful. I've found a new dance teacher. He'll teach hip hop and some other things the kids like to do."

"Hip hop? Really?" Brenna followed Gram out to the kitchen. "What does that involve?"

Trix trailed them with only half an ear on their conversation.

"B-boying which is the new term for breakdancing. Then there's locking and popping, funk, up rock, liquid dance, and boogaloo. Next week there could be more."

Trix had said all she wanted to say about Jon Carpenter, and she hoped Brenna didn't mention him again. If she insisted they were just client and contractor, her family wouldn't listen anyway. If they decided he was the man for her, then she didn't have a hope of convincing them otherwise. Best to keep them guessing.

Still, it would be nice to talk with him again. He was busy drawing up plans right now. It was good that her project was his priority. He'd made that clear. She wondered if he'd get his son involved as he'd mentioned on the way to their vehicles after lunch. Men liked the idea of passing on a business to their kids and Jon would be no exception.

The day after his lunch with Trix, Jon stood at his son's bedroom door waiting to be acknowledged while Ben practiced dance moves he'd seen a million times. The arm movements, robotic, the legs stiff. But put together, there was a grace Jon appreciated.

Lunch with Trix had been time well spent, in his opinion. He couldn't remember being as relaxed in years. She calmed him in some way. Her smiles were genuine and kind without being full of pity.

He was sick of seeing pitying smiles all over town. Half of him had wanted to move away from Dickens when Melody died. The other half stuck to his word to keep the kids in school here with their friends. Deathbed requests were impossible to refuse, and he'd made it work. And now, he got to work with a woman who had no memories of him being married and caring for his sick wife. Maybe that's why being with Trix refreshed him.

He assumed the calming effect she had on him would pass as he worked on the barn. She'd change her plans, her mind, the colors she wanted and all the myriad details as the project took shape. They'd have discussions about the budget, her changes to the plans, and the ensuing changes to the budget. Things could get heated as they sometimes did on a big job.

When Ben turned around and caught sight of him at the door, he stopped and tugged out his earplugs. "Sorry, I didn't see you there."

"Nice moves. You're good," he said. "I want to offer you a job."

"Huh?" Ben tilted his head in surprise.

"I hoped you'd want to learn the business. Working on Ms. Warden's barn would be a great opportunity. Easier than doing a full tear down of a dump." He crossed his arms over his chest. "We'll know what to expect and the work will move fast. You'd learn a lot."

Ben frowned deeply and shook his head.

"It's time, Ben." Jon firmed his tone. What did he think? That money flowed from a faucet? He saw the long hours Jon worked some days. He tried not to loom over the kid, but all the calm he'd had fled as he recognized a stubborn tilt to Ben's chin. Loom wasn't exactly right since Ben's height was quickly catching up his, but still.

"I've already got a job," Ben said, exasperated. "I can work Saturdays and after school. Set my own hours if I want."

Those were the hours Jon wanted from him. He frowned. "This is the first I've heard of a job."

"Because I just got it. Like, today." His chin jutted and Jon knew exactly where he got the look. He was staring at himself at sixteen.

But since he was trying to listen better, Jon took the bait. "That sounds like a dream job. Where is it?"

"Tiny Tim's Dance Studio."

He shook his head. "What'll you be doing?"

"Teaching dance. The stuff kids are into. Hip Hop. Not all the old fogie stuff like the tango and rumba or tap."

"You loved tap. When you quit you were miserable," he blurted. Awkward. He recognized how smooth Ben's moves were. But teaching? That seemed a stretch.

The jut of his chin disappeared as Ben softened his expression. "It wasn't quitting tap that made me sad."

That stopped Jon's argument cold. All the things he could say flew out of his head. "Of course it wasn't. Your mom would be happy you found another way to dance. That's a good sign, right?"

"Sure." Ben walked toward him, reached out a hand and softly closed the door in his face. Jon placed his palm on the door and listened through the wood. He heard footfalls in a rhythm he recognized. Ben had been dancing this way for a long time. A year? Maybe more. Why hadn't he noticed? Had grief cocooned him from seeing his own kids?

He could push the door open and take up the discussion again. He could try to push the kid into working with him, but Ben needed this separate life that made him happy. Jon couldn't stand in his way.

Still, Jon was no quitter. "Got any buddies who want to learn construction?" He asked through the door. The idea of teaching a willing student still appealed to him. He had skills he'd like to pass on to someone, if that someone wanted to learn.

"No. I gotta practice now."

"What about kids from school?" But he got no reply.

Trix might know someone. Funny how she was the first adult he wanted to ask. Silly, because she'd only been back in Dickens a short while. She had no nephews Ben's age. Asking her could be a dead end. Still, she was a good listener and had great suggestions.

Chapter Six

After striking out with Ben, Jon left the house, walked to his truck, and climbed in. A glance at the gas gauge gave him pause. He'd filled up on the weekend and he hadn't been anywhere outside of Dickens. Not even out to the highway where the box stores sat like soldiers at a campfire. He tapped the gauge and frowned.

His phone rang. It was Blair. "Hi, sweetheart. What got you up early on a Saturday morning?"

"I need to go shopping. Can you drive me?"

Shopping to Blair meant an hours-long marathon of running from store to store digging through sale racks. Melody had taught her to buy off-season and clearance when she could get it. As long as Jon paid her clothing bills, Blair agreed to wear less-than the newest styles.

"I've got to run out to the barn to talk to Ms. Warden. I'll be home in an hour or so."

"Good. I'll be ready."

He'd give her an hour and a half.

Trix sat in Jon's pickup, on the town square in front of the hardware store. She'd picked out a new lock for the barn door. Jon had suggested a fancy one with a security code, so they'd come to check them out. She warmed her toes under the blast of the heater. It was time to change into warmer sneakers as the weather cooled.

For twenty minutes they'd discussed all they'd needed to talk about for the renovations. Time to wind down. They needed to deal with the rest of their respective days, but she was loath to say goodbye. Being with Jon settled her and with all the work and details she had to deal with, feeling settled gave her a respite. She dug around for a new impersonal topic.

"Have you noticed that Christmas decorations are going up all over town?"

He nodded. "They take down the spooky stuff and replace it with Christmas wreaths on the lampposts immediately. One smooth operation they manage after the kids go home after trick or treating."

"Have you ever attended the tree lighting ceremony?"

"Every year. But I doubt either of my kids will want to be seen with me this year. I probably won't bother. It meant a lot to Melody that we all go together, but Blair and Ben prefer to hang out with their friends."

"My whole family attends. You're welcome to join us."

"Thanks, but it's weeks away. I'll see when I get there," he said.

She felt a smidge embarrassed for asking. "I shouldn't have asked. Forget it," she said with a gentle smile. She'd done it again. Made him remember his life with his dead wife. He must miss her terribly at Christmas. Especially when it came to family events they attended. She studied the view of the town square, trying to come up with a less hurtful topic.

"I guess I should go..."

"Speaking of your family..." he trailed off at the same time she did. But he settled against the driver's door, apparently ready to talk. Good. She'd have a few more minutes of feeling comfortable and connected. A balm.

"Yes?"

"Your grandmother just stole away my son."

She chuckled. "Some older fellas around Dickens may think she's a hottie, but that's a big stretch," she teased. Stan, the town clerk, had asked after Gram more than once.

"Funny." His lips twitched. "I'm sure she's a real catch, being a dancer and all, and I remember how nice she is, but that's not what I mean. She's hired him out from under me."

"You wanted him with you during the renos." And then she remembered. "*He's* the one she hired to teach Hip Hop?"

"Oh, you knew?"

"I heard her telling Brenna about new classes, but I was wrapped up in my own problems. I didn't catch the teacher's name." She frowned. "Do you need me to plead your case, so she'll put him off?" She hated to interfere, but if Jon needed Ben, then she'd talk to Gram.

He shook his head. "I'll find another kid somewhere who wants to learn. I can go talk to the shop teacher at the high school for a likely candidate for after school and weekends."

"Whew, thanks. I'd have said something, but I'm happy I don't have to. Asking at the high school is a great idea."

"I'm glad he wants to work and if this makes him happy, then he'll stick with it for a good while."

"Teachers come and go," she said. "Last Christmas, Jett showed up in Dickens and taught Tango. It was a cover so he could find Billie Adamson. He ended up falling for Brenna and now, they're married, and Billie's invention is helping the environment."

"I'd heard about Jett and Billie, of course, but not the bit about teaching the Tango. That spices the story up quite a bit."

It was her turn to laugh. "You've heard what they say about Dickens. At Christmas, miracles happen."

"I hadn't heard that, but then, I wasn't raised here." He tilted his head and looked askance. "Are you saying you're hoping for a Christmas miracle with your renos?"

She warmed through at his intent stare. "I don't believe I need a miracle when I have you." Jon Carpenter probably *was* the miracle.

Red flashes appeared on his cheeks. "That's a lot of faith you have there."

"Maybe, but now that I know you better, I doubt it's misplaced." She felt the baby kick and shifted quickly. She patted her stomach over the spot. "That was a good one."

"You felt a kick?" His eyes lit up with interest.

"It's funny but sometimes now there's a whole series rather than one here and there."

He nodded as if he understood. Of course he did. He was a father twice.

"Is it more active at different times of the day?"

"Yes."

"Melody told me that it felt like Blair was twanging on the muscle that controlled her leg. Like a guitar string, she said." His words came fast as his memories spilled out. "Anyway," he waved his hand. "She pulled over to the side of the road until the twanging stopped because she wasn't sure she could drive with all the twitching down her leg."

"That's funny. I've had some odd feelings too."

"It was only that one time, but Blair's always liked to be in control. I wonder if that was the beginning?"

"Could be." They shared a smile, his in memory and hers in happy anticipation.

"If you don't mind me saying, the baby's father is missing out on a lot."

"More than you know," she responded vaguely. Dale deserved to be a vague memory, not a sharp, painful one. "Well...I have a lot of artists to talk with today. I need to get commitments from them, that way I can count how many large stalls I'll need. May I get back to you?"

"I'd suggest you make the decision and offer them what you have. That'll save time and money."

"I get it. By doing that, I maintain control of the space." She liked that. Her building, her choice. "Okay." She nodded. "I'll call and feel them out about what they'll require without making promises. Then I'll decide and tell you what to plan for."

He nodded and smiled broadly. "I'll advise my crew we're starting ASAP."

"Sorry about Ben not joining you."

"His choice. I'll manage."

With that, she opened the door and climbed out. "Thanks for all the advice. I've never done anything like this before." Never been in charge, never had to make choices that effected other people this way.

"Thanks for listening to the advice. Not all my clients do." He winked at her and buckled his seatbelt.

She closed the door and stepped back to let him drive off. For a second, she wished she were still in the truck with him.

Foolish, foolish thought. What man in his right mind would want to hang out with a pregnant woman?

Chapter Seven

Jon checked Trix out in his rearview. For a moment there, he'd wanted to invite her to spend the afternoon with him.

Doing nothing. Hanging out. Maybe watching a movie on his couch. She'd prop her feet up on his lap while he gave her a foot rub. Pregnant women appreciated foot rubs. They were on par with doing household chores without being asked.

What a fool he was being. The man who'd left her behind would come to his senses and claim her anytime now. He turned his gaze to the road, saw the cross street and turned right toward home.

Blair needed a ride to the outdoor mall. At least she was old enough to be there without a parent. Melody had missed this milestone and had felt obligated to hang around while Blair had met with a gaggle of girlfriends, whose moms also hung around, pretending not to be there. The moms circled and swooped and kept a distant eye on their daughters when they were twelve.

Melody would be proud of him for letting Blair fledge. She'd be proud of the young woman Blair was becoming.

He picked her up as promised and on the twenty-minute drive to the highway interchange that fed the mall, they chatted about school, boys, and Ben.

"You're okay with Ben getting a job?" she asked.

"Tiny Tim's beat me to him. I wanted him to join me over at Ms. Warden's barn reno, but he'd rather teach dance."

She nodded but didn't comment.

"Were you aware that he wanted to teach?"

Shrug. "He's good. He has a lot of followers, and they send him messages to get him to show them his tips. Basically, he was already teaching online."

"Can't people make money that way?"

"Sure, but it's a lot of work. A real time-suck. This way, he works the hours he sets himself."

"A lot of work, huh?"

"Big influencers are working constantly. There's not a part of their day they're not focused on what they do."

"You've put thought into this."

She gave him a sidelong glance. "People assume they can do makeup tutorials and make millions. It's way more than that."

He pulled into the parking lot and rolled to a stop near the front door of her favorite store. He spied her new friends standing by the door. Two of them were smoking. One vaped. He didn't recognize any of them.

"When did you start hanging out with smokers?"

"They're trying to quit. I've told them they have to before they get hooked. But it's hard, okay? It's hard to quit. They're trying!" With that, she opened her door and hopped down. She slammed the door shut and stepped off, shoulders squared and head high.

When she approached the group, the two with cigarettes dropped them and stamped them out. The one vaping slipped her device into her pocket. All three of them looked guilty.

He'd love to hear the lecture they were getting from Blair. Satisfied that she was a leader, not a follower, he headed home. He needed to hit his drafting table to lay out some plans. On the drive he called his crew and gave them the good news that they had work through the fall.

Trix finished her last call of the day. Faith Jones was a coup for the market and had been Trix's first choice for a crafter. Faith created marvelous wall hangings from different natural materials like lamb's wool, reclaimed cotton, Alpaca fiber, and driftwood pieces. Faith was doing well in galleries, but she saw the advantage of having her own booth where she could talk directly to customers. Still, talking to customers was the part she hated, and she needed to be convinced.

Gram had been gone all day because Saturday was the busiest day for the dance studio. Ever since Trix had talked with Jon about Ben teaching at Tiny Tim's she'd been consumed with an idea.

Now that her phone calls were completed, Trix couldn't resist heading over to Tiny Tim's to check out how Ben was doing with his first day teaching. She wouldn't introduce herself, of course, but she could wander into her grandmother's cubby-hole of an office and observe. That would indicate to him that she had the right to be at the studio and by not telling him her name, she wouldn't raise the alarm that she'd report back to his father.

She hadn't told Jon her plan because it hadn't formed until she'd finished with the phone calls to her artists. *Her artists.* The phrase warmed her. Only two had changed their minds. Which was fine. She'd be smart to have an empty stall or two for when word got out about this opportunity. Positive she'd missed some talented people who were shy about showing their work, she looked forward to being the one to help them build their business.

Faith would be a great boost. She was well-respected in the crafting community and if she was a success, then more crafters would want space.

She now understood the joy that her Manhattan gallery gave Cecilia. Helping an artist be discovered would be wonderful and Trix looked forward to their successes.

The drive to the town square took five minutes. She couldn't find a parking spot, so she drove into the alley that led to a lot behind the stores. She should call Jon to share her plan. They could enjoy a few quiet moments while she reported what she saw.

A father would appreciate insider knowledge. She called his number, feeling like a private detective, but in a good way; not a spying-for-a-parent way.

"Hi there," he answered, sounding gravelly and um...hot. At least to her ears.

Darn hormones. She'd heard some pregnant women had heightened lust, but a simple greeting shouldn't get her engines revved. He'd be disgusted if he knew the roly-poly baby vessel was lusting after him.

"What can I do for you?" he prompted when she still hadn't spoken.

"Oh, Jon," she breathed. *Get a grip!* "You'll tell me not to do this."

"Do what?"

"Wander into my grandmother's dance studio this afternoon."

"You can do that?"

"Of course. We've all taken and/or taught lessons there as we grew up. My favorite to teach was the rumba."

"Not hip-hop?" he teased.

"No."

"When are you going? Will Ben know who you are, because—."

"I won't tell him. But I'll report back to you if you'd like."

There was a pause as he considered her offer. "I'll be there in half an hour. Will that give you enough time?"

"Absolutely. Where shall we meet? I'm parked in the lot behind the stores."

"I'll find you there. I have some plans to show you anyway. Preliminary of course. We could look at them over dinner at Antonelli's."

A thrill shot through her. Totally inappropriate, but still...she was a woman after all.

"Okay," she squeaked. Did she squeak? No, she couldn't have. She was a thirty-seven-year-old woman and women her age didn't squeak at casual dinner invitations.

They did if the man asking was as good looking as Jon Carpenter. She shut down the foolish thought. Hard.

Then, she scampered out of her car and over to the back door of Tiny Tim's Dance Studio. She hurried up the stairs and when she reached the door, she smoothed her hair and entered quietly.

The studio was packed with people of all ages. She presumed the teacher was Ben because a teenage boy was at the front of the full class of thirty. Three rows of ten people followed his steps: some well, some faltering, but they were all smiling.

Jon should see this, but it would distract Ben if his father showed up out of the blue. Not to mention Ben's loss of street cred. She grinned at the phrase. From the office door, Gram waved her over.

With stealth and years of practice avoiding disruption, Trix sidled down the wall toward the back of the class, then hotfooted it across to where her grandmother waited.

"Hi," she said softly. "The turnout is amazing."

"A great response," Gram agreed. "They lined up before the ballet class was over."

"The teacher is my contractor's son. He doesn't know that I hired his father for the barn renovations."

"Are you spying?" The twinkle in her grandmother's eye made Trix grin back.

"Just this once." She raised her phone for a quick photo. "Jon will want to see this." Then she added a short video, too. She immediately pocketed her phone when she was finished.

"Aren't you sending those?" Gram asked with an innocent expression.

Trix frowned. She hadn't considered emailing the images to Jon. That would have been simpler, but less fun.

"No, he's downstairs. He has plans he's drawn up to show me, and I thought he'd like a peek at how his son was doing in here," she explained.

At her grandmother's raised brow she continued. "We're eating at Antonelli's," she added brisk and businesslike. "So don't hold dinner for me."

Gram waved her out. "Great, more Shepherd's pie for me. Bring home a loaf of garlic bread, please." Antonelli's had a sideline selling fresh baked loaves, and the locals took full advantage when they dined there.

A few minutes later, Jon stood close beside her, looking at her phone. His expression moved through surprise, delight, and pride. She could feel his fierce heat through her puffy jacket and his shearling. She drank in his scent. "Unbelievable," he said. "Look at the crowd." He sounded awestruck. "Ben's good. He's been practicing for ages. But, to see this? Amazing."

"That's capacity," she explained. They stood side by side, shoulders brushing as he looked at her phone. His shoulders hunched around her protectively as he took the phone for a closer look. His fingers warmed her as they touched hers. He zoomed in on the screen, bringing his son into the frame more clearly.

"The go-fer position I offered can't compete with that," he said proudly. "He's having fun."

"I assume his after-school classes will be just as busy," she said, excited for father and son. "He'll make decent money."

"As long as he keeps up his grades, I'm all for it."

Chapter Eight

Jon followed Trix's sporty hatchback to Antonelli's, pride in his son burning in his chest. Some dads might be disappointed in a kid who loved to dance. His own would've frowned at the idea, having had some old-fashioned notions about what was manly and what wasn't. He'd expected Jon to follow him into a trade and Jon had been happy with that choice. It had been natural for Jon to think Ben might want to learn at his side through high school, but Ben was right to choose his own path.

He was also pleased that Ben had gone to Mrs. Moore on his own. He'd made his decision and acted on it.

When he'd learned that his plans for college had suddenly changed with Melody's unexpected pregnancy, Jon had understood what his parents expected from him. He'd been happy to step up, to go to work and provide for his young family.

Melody's parents were different from his. When she'd got pregnant, they hadn't pressured for marriage, convinced that traditions were constrictions to free thinking. No, it had been Jon who'd wanted to 'do the right thing,' but not because of convention, not because of his parent's expectations. But because he'd loved Melody. She was the only girl for him.

The only girl.

Tonight it was a woman he followed to a romantic restaurant that had linen on the tables, soft lighting, and candles. He shook his head. A woman who was twice Melody's age when he'd married her.

This attraction to Trix had come out of the blue and if he were honest, he didn't want it. Maybe he was attracted more to her circumstance than the woman herself. Maybe he felt like this because she was pregnant, alone, and being brave about it. She was an admirable, talented, determined woman.

But he'd already married a pregnant girl. He understood what it was like to have a new baby in a brand-new marriage. It was tough. There was no time to be a couple. And then, they'd done it again right away with Blair.

This feeling he had for Trix was no more than friendly appreciation. Once he was finished with the work at the barn, they'd go their separate ways, and their mutual interest would slip away. As it should.

He'd build a cradle for the baby as a parting gift. He liked the idea, and he was sure Trix would appreciate the gesture.

At dinner, he'd allude to the idea that they'd work well together during the project but that would be the end of it.

Trix was smart. She'd take the hint.

"I'm sorry I'm not dressed for this place. I'd've worn my best jeans if I'd known we were going fancy," Jon quipped. He held Trix's chair for her, aware how much like a date this looked. He hung his shearling on the back of his chair and ran his fingers through his hair when he sat across from her.

She cozied up to the table. "Hey," she said, her voice full of humor, "this was your idea, not mine."

"I didn't feel like having the regulars at Dorrit's telling tales about you." He took his seat across from her and set his tube of rolled plans on the floor beside the table.

"Worried about my good name?" she teased.

"Something like that." Nobody believed her child was his, but it would be fodder for the gossip mill if —

"Trix Warden! What a surprise," a feminine voice boomed across the room. "And with a handsome man, too."

Trix craned her neck to see who'd called to them. "Marva. Nice to see you."

An older woman sailed across the room like a square-rigged whaler, dressed in a parrot's colors. Purple and orange from head to toe, Trix's friend enveloped her in a hug and a fog of flowery scent. "So good to see you. I'm here to help Jett with some business and to spend time with Harry."

A man stood behind Marva, a dull brown sparrow in comparison to his date. But his eyes were alight with pride, his face wreathed in a smile.

"And who's this?" Marva demanded, staring pointedly at Jon, her eyes wide. "The father, I hope."

Jon felt heat rise from his neck to his face. His shoulders squared of their own accord.

"Marva," Trix said in a stern voice. She shook her head to tame the woman's blather. "This is my contractor, Jon Carpenter. Meet Marva, a dear friend to us all except when she runs her mouth."

Marva laughed off the cheeky criticism. "I love you all, you know that."

"Marva works for Jett now." Trix's affection filled her voice. "He coaxed her out of retirement.

"Last Christmas, Jett taught me to tango," Marva added. "How else could I catch the eye of my Harry?"

Harry cleared his throat and ducked his head. "She's a pistol." He took Marva's hand and placed it on his arm.

"Nice to meet you both," Jon said to move things along. He picked up his menu. Small talk was not his strong suit.

"Harry, how are you?" Trix asked, as she cocked her eyebrow at Jon. More cheek.

"Better now that Marva's here." It was clear the man was infatuated with the loud, brassy woman with orange and purple streaks in her hair. And it was also clear that Marva was a favorite person in Trix's life.

The banter threatened to continue so Jon held up the tube that contained the plans he'd drawn. "We're here to go over some drawings."

"Of course you are," Marva declared in a saucy tone that said she didn't believe a word. "Have a lovely date. Harry and I will leave you to it."

Trix looked pained at the woman's obvious ploy but could do nothing but smile and wave the other couple off. After they stepped away, she leaned across the table. "Marva will report back to Jett and Brenna the first chance she gets. And then, they'll tell the rest of the family." She rolled her eyes. "But I did tell my grandmother not to expect me for dinner and that we were coming here."

Jon looked out the window and saw Marva highlighted by a light over the entrance. "She's on her phone right now," he said with a sigh. "Nothing moves faster than gossip."

"Sorry, I guess this does look kind of like a date." She smoothed her hand across the linen-covered tabletop. "I'd blow out the candle, but they're battery operated tealights." She picked it out of the glass bowl. "Maybe I can turn it off."

"Stop. It won't matter now, and Marva seemed determined to see what she wanted anyway, no matter what we said."

"At least I told Gram we were meeting to discuss plans. I suppose we should get to it." She gave him a game smile.

Jon asked a passing waiter to move them to a table for four. Once they settled there, he opened his canister and then pulled out two sheets of rolled drafting paper. He unrolled them on the other half of the table. He pointed at the drawing on the top sheet.

"This is the main floor and the next sheet beneath this one is your office in the loft. Eventually, we could add smaller booths upstairs or create storage for the artists if they need it. But that can come with time."

"Let's focus on the main floor first," she said on a slowly exhaled breath. Excitement stirred the space between them, and he grinned.

The server appeared with an ice bucket containing a non-alcoholic bottle of sparkling cider. "Compliments of Marva and Harry," she explained as she set down two flutes.

"Lovely, I'll thank her later," Trix responded drily and gave him a wink.

He chuckled and lifted the bottle from the bucket. "Imported from Maine. The label says it's their best, award-winning cider."

"Ooh, nice."

"But next time we need to have a meeting, we should probably do take-out and eat at the barn."

"Agreed," she said with a nod. "This dating gossip could get out of hand. I'm sorry about her crack about you being the baby's father." She looked guilty, as if it were her fault Marva probed.

The stories were probably already out of hand but didn't want to add to her guilt. "There are lots of reasons we should meet privately. We're strictly business. Friendly, but business."

"Absolutely," she agreed with a steady green-hazel look that threatened to pull him in. "Once the barn is complete, I'll be having this baby and you'll move on to another project." She sighed and patted her bump.

"You think you're busy now? This ain't nothin' sweetheaaarttt," he drawled. "I'm glad the babies, diapers, daycare expenses, and being stuck at home are all behind me."

"You paint a rosy picture," she said drily, and then took a big swallow of cider to wash down the words.

"In five years, I'll be lucky to see Ben and Blair on holidays. I don't expect either of them to return to Dickens after college. It's a great town, beautiful even, but it's no place to launch a career."

Her eyes went wide. "I hope it's a good place to launch a market."

"I believe it is, but you have life experience and an established following through the gallery in New York. You're not a kid starting out."

"I'm no kid," she said. "I'm downright geriatric. My doctor and biology says so." Her lips pinched until white showed at the corners.

"I didn't mean to—."

She cut off his apology with a wave of her hand. "I'm sorry to make this about me. I blame the hormones."

"You have a lot on your plate."

"I know where I'll be in five years," she commented as she read the menu. "Here, wrangling a kindergartner. But what about you? Being an empty nester by then you can live anywhere or do anything."

He smiled. "Melody dreamed of traveling the world," he admitted. "She'd say, no kids, 'just us.'"

"Sounds fun and breezy."

"We missed a lot of easy breezy fun stuff in our early years."

"You had a family right away. You were, what? Twenty?"

"Nineteen for Ben, twenty for Blair. They came early, but I can make up for that lost time soon." He looked off to the middle distance, remembering some of his and Melody's plans. "I could backpack through Europe or around Australia. Or I could go to college to become an architect." He looked into Trix's interested gaze and faltered. *Or he could be here.*

"Freedom has a nice ring to it," she said softly.

Chapter Nine

Monday morning, Jon backed out of his driveway and heard a clatter, felt a lurch, and slammed to a stop. He shut off the engine and jumped out of his truck to see what had happened. The crumpled back bumper had detached as his truck had reversed onto the road.

If he hadn't heard the clatter and stopped immediately he'd have run it over.

He saw red and spun for the front door.

"BEN!" He hollered as he slammed into the entrance hall. "Get your butt outside. NOW!"

Ben ran then skidded to a halt in his socks in front of him. "What happened?" His eyes went wide as saucers.

"Don't play dumb. Get out there!"

"Dad—"

Jon was already back outside. A minute later, as Jon was opening his tailgate both of his children, looking pensive, arrived. Blair was still in her robe and slippers while Ben, the early riser, was dressed. His face was painted by guilt, while hers looked frightened.

"Blair, it's okay," Jon assured her. "This is between me and your brother." He swung toward Ben. "Your brother, who's been taking my truck out at night without my permission, knowledge, or a driver's license!" The more he said, the louder he got until he saw a neighbor across the street had stopped to watch the show.

Jon waved to Fred Macintyre, who nodded and grinned.

"Teens," the neighbor called as he opened his car door. "This too shall pass."

Jon took a deep breath that didn't calm him. The Macintyres had a boy who'd entered rehab last year and come out the other side. He dreaded to think about how Ben's joyriding might have ended.

Jon narrowed his gaze at his son. "This behavior had better pass and darn soon. I noticed the gas gauge was down the other day, but I assumed I'd lost track of what day I filled up. But I didn't get the day wrong, did I?"

Ben shrugged. "No?"

Blair shifted. "Dad..."

"Blair, go on inside and get ready for school. You're walking today because I have to get the truck into a body shop. And guess whose new job will pay for it?"

Ben blanched and glared at his father.

Blair flashed her brother a look of sympathy and went inside.

"Won't insurance cover it?" Ben whined.

"I'm supposed to report that my unlicensed son was joyriding in my work vehicle and now they should cover the cost of repairs?" He stormed to the back of the truck and surveyed the damage again. "Did you back into something? Or did someone rear end you?"

Trix listened carefully as Jon grumbled. "Ben couldn't or wouldn't answer me." She sympathized. Raising teens was tough at the best of times, but his two had lost their mom and the family was struggling. Maybe Ben was acting out.

They were in the barn, an hour later than planned because of Jon's interrupted morning. The plans were spread out on a folding table she'd brought in. Four folding chairs, an insulated jug of coffee and a lunch cooler with sandwiches and fruit to share sat nearby. She'd had hopes of a picnic for lunch. Silly, because Jon was too wound up about his son to notice the food. "He claims he has no clue how the back end got hit," he explained.

"Maybe it happened when he wasn't with the truck? Could he have parked and left it somewhere? You said you didn't notice until the bumper fell off, so it stands to reason he wouldn't see it in the dark." She tossed out questions because she had no answers and Jon needed to vent his frustration. Better with her than his half-grown son. Teenage boys could be volatile and a man's truck sacrosanct. "Could he have lent it to a friend?"

"I didn't ask, and he didn't say. He didn't offer any explanation and that made me too angry to think clearly." He frowned, considering. "He could have covered for someone." His expression lightened. "That's the kind of kid he is. Loyal."

"Loyalty's great unless it goes too far," she said softly.

Jon nodded. "I wish you'd been there. I could have used some backup. Blair felt sorry for him, so she was no help. It felt like two against one until I sent her into the house." He huffed through his nose. "The thing is, I understand him wanting to drive. Most teenage boys take their dad's car out for a spin at some point. But most don't come home damaged." He swallowed hard. "What if it had been a more serious accident?"

"Get him driving lessons," she blurted. Technically he was venting, not asking for advice but she'd offered it before, and he'd been okay with her speaking up.

He glared. His eyes darkened with roiling emotions she didn't want to pinpoint.

"You keep up that glare and I'll be shaking in my boots," she said. She raised both eyebrows and waited.

They shared a glare, but he blinked first and then looked to the ceiling for a count of two. When he looked at her again, he'd calmed. "I'm supposed to reward him with lessons?"

"It's not a reward." She shook her head. "It's prevention. He should be a competent driver when he's the behind the wheel of your truck. He needs insurance. And he needs assurance that you won't freak cut on him for being a normal teenager."

He pinched his lips and gave one brusque nod. "I'll call a driving school today and get whatever he needs to get his learner's permit. But he's paying for the repairs to my truck and his lessons."

"Of course." She nodded and waited. Soon, he'd return to the reason he was here. "Will your crew arrive soon?" Work was to start today.

Jon ran his hand down his cheeks and then dragged in a deep breath. "Yes. Let's get this done." Twin flags of color painted his cheekbones. "I shouldn't dump my family stuff on you. I do it all the time."

"I've been told I have one of those personalities. The kind that makes people confide."

"I'm not sure how you do it, but I always get a different perspective after talking to you." He smiled and his gaze snagged hers for a long moment.

This time, she blinked first.

"Now, how many stalls will you want in the ladies' room?" he asked.

"Two downstairs, including an accessible stall. Could you rough in plumbing for a two-piece washroom upstairs?"

"I can move your office closer to the water supply to make it easier." He pointed to the large sink and hoses against the back wall. "The public washrooms will go there."

"Can we keep that sink there for the artists? They'll have tools or equipment to clean. It would be handy to have a utility sink."

"Done." The sound of vehicles outside heralded the arrival of Jon's crew. "The guys are here. If you want to stay to hear my instructions, you're welcome. Once we start work this will be a hardhat area and you'll need to wear appropriate footwear." His tone was all business and she rose to stand as he did.

"I'll come back later for lunch. I made enough to feed an army." She waved at the cooler she'd brought.

He shook his head to decline her offer. "I'll eat as I work to make up for my late arrival. Don't worry about feeding me."

With that, the door opened and three men in hardhats, toolbelts, and work boots arrived.

"That's a lot of plaid," she muttered but Jon was out of earshot as he walked toward the new arrivals. Just as well. She doubted he'd understand her reaction to men in toolbelts. She waved a hand in front of her face and waddled over to meet the men.

After a round of handshakes and congratulations about the baby, she left them to their work. She'd considered staying to hear what Jon had to say, but a call of nature took precedence. All that talk of washrooms had woken the baby who'd taken the opportunity to press against her bladder. Sometimes the little punkin did jumping jacks.

Could she make it to Gram's house? Doubtful. She'd head for the dance studio instead since it was on the common and closer.

She was thrilled to leave her dreams in the hands of Jon Carpenter. He was serious, dedicated, honest, and straightforward. He cared for his family and his business. And by extension, his clients. Which meant her.

She hoped his son would get through this rough patch. Given time, she felt certain Ben would grow into a fine young man.

After all, he had a wonderful man to look up to and emulate.

When Trix arrived at Tiny Tim's, Gram was teaching a rumba class. Two couples, clearly beginners. She hung up her jacket and scarf and gave Gram a quick wave before scuttling into the ladies' room.

As she re-entered the studio, she heard Gram talking. "The rumba is originally from Cuba, which means there's a lot of hip action. The dance is meant to show the man's pursuit of a woman."

The women students laughed. In their forties, they looked like a group of friends.

"Take the closed position please." Gram demonstrated with her hands up. "Chin level should be comfortable for you." She clicked her remote control and the music rose. "Remember, it's quick, quick, slow."

Trix nodded, remembering her lessons from long ago. She wasn't sure the baby would allow for a lot of 'hip action', but she'd love to find out. With Jon. Her smile broadened as she forced herself not to laugh out loud at the image of her belly swaying two beats behind her hips.

Jon would make some droll remark and then hold her in his arms to dance.

The man was never far from her mind, but these fantasies were useless. He'd made it plain where his future lay and it wasn't in Dickens. He would not be the man in her life.

And they would never dance the rumba.

No, Jon would be traveling the world in a handful of years, and she'd be here, building a life with her child. Maybe there'd be a man to go along with that life, but it wouldn't be Jon.

Her mind was clear as crystal on where their friendship was headed, but her heart seemed muddy on the concept of eventually saying goodbye.

In the meantime, they made a wonderful team as they built her studio and talked about his children. It was true what she'd said about people confiding in her. She had one of those faces and a calm demeanor. She also tried not to judge, which went a long way when people were confessing.

Still, it felt nice to be the one leaning on someone. Jon listened to her when she asked questions, and answered her in a direct, truthful manner. If her idea for the remodel wasn't easily workable, he explained why and sometimes, offered an alternative. It was heaven to be heard and to be treated as an equal, even if her understanding of carpentry and building was sketchy.

Dale had never wanted to listen to her. Not to her dreams, or aspirations, or disappointments. Eventually, she'd stopped talking about them. After that it had been a short hop to giving them up completely.

In her marriage she'd denied her artistic nature for far too long, settling into a boring, thankless banking job that had no future. But Dale had convinced her they needed the money more than she needed to express herself with painting.

Sure, she could offer levelheaded advice to others, but she'd been unable to see how far off track she'd gotten. Her cousins had hinted that Dale could be more supportive of her art. When she'd tossed her paints, easel, and brushes, they'd quit mentioning her art. She'd taken their silence as support for her decision.

She couldn't have been more wrong. In the time since her divorce, Brenna and Kayley had been behind her all the way. If they learned about her conflicted feelings for Jon, they'd never leave her alone to sort them out. They'd like Jon because he was great, and they'd be frustrated on her behalf if things went the way Trix believed they would. She couldn't handle their disappointment, or their pity because of another failed relationship.

So her cousins would remain in the dark. Gram, too. Whatever road she and Jon were on, was their journey, no one else's.

B y four o'clock, Jon was pleased with the work done, and after brief instructions to his crew he headed to the high school to have a conversation with the shop class teacher. An hour after school closed there were still lots of vehicles in the staff parking lot. The student lot looked full, too.

The fall was football season and when he climbed out of his truck, he heard the evidence from the far side of the school. The team was running drills. A wash of memory rolled through his mind as he recalled his time as a Puma back in his Vermont high school. He grinned and headed for the front entrance.

A passing student gave him directions to the shop class, and he ventured down the hall. The door was open and the sound of students talking drew him in. The teacher saw him, pushed his safety glasses to his forehead and greeted him.

"How can I help you?"

He introduced himself and shook hands with James Dillon, a man in his fifties. From the happy faces and excited chatter, it was clear his students liked him and enjoyed the time they spent in here. "Are all these kids in detention?"

The teacher shook his head. "I prefer to think of Shop as a reward, not a punishment."

"It was certainly a reward for me," Jon admitted with a smile. He passed Mr. Dillon his business card.

Dillon smiled. "Some of these kids are perfectionists and can't leave a perfectly good hall table alone." He raised his voice to be heard over the chatter. "Deacon, I told you, your mom'll love it."

"But the leg isn't right yet." The teen went back to work with the wood lathe.

Mr. Dillon shook his head and winked at Jon. "The kid's a natural."

"Maybe he'd like to join my crew after school and on Saturdays. I'm looking for a bright kid to help over at Scott's barn. It's a full renovation. I'd need him until the end of the year, but if he's an apt student it could be for longer."

Mr. Dillon called Deacon over and presented the offer.

Deacon looked enthusiastic as he listened closely, but then regret filled his features. "I can't take it, Mr. Carpenter, I'm sorry. After the hour I put in here I need to get home to watch my sisters. My mom works shifts and she'll need to sleep."

"Thanks, Deacon. I understand. But the offer will be open anytime things change for you. Mr. Dillon speaks highly of you."

"Thanks! Maybe in the summer? If the hours are flexible." He looked hopeful and Jon nodded.

"Here's my card. Keep it and call me when you can."

"I will." He stared at the card with a smile, and then slipped it into his pocket. "I gotta go now. Thanks, again."

After he left, the teacher nodded. "He'd be great to have on your team. He's a good student and willing to learn."

"That's more than I can say for my son Ben. He has no interest in the family business. That's why I'm here. I figured this was a good place to look for a likely candidate."

"I teach Ben. I guess that means you're also Blair's dad."

"Yes," he said, confused. "But how do you know her? Do you teach something else?" Or maybe he'd seen her in detention. He suspected she'd had a few he didn't know about. His own parents hadn't known about most of his.

"No." Mr. Dillon smiled and nodded. "Maybe you're looking at the wrong child to introduce to carpentry. Blair's been coming in since last year. I believe she had a crush at the time and followed him in. But she took an interest in woodwork. The crush is long gone, but she's here Wednesdays, like clockwork. Sometimes Thursday, too."

Jon shook head. Shook it again as he tried to take in what the teacher was saying about his daughter. At least the crush was over. "Carpentry? My Blair?"

Mr. Dillon propped his butt against his desk and crossed his arms over his chest. "I take it she never said. She's good at inlay. She's made chessboards and other board games. Her backgammon board is right there on the wall."

Jon turned to look. The board hung, framed, beside the large window. He walked over to take a close look.

"She's never said anything," he said. "Never looked at my tools." A memory came to him. "Not since she was a little girl." He studied the board. The long, narrow triangles that made up the board were perfectly aligned and even. The finish was perfect. "She liked to pretend to work with screwdrivers and hammers. She helped me make a small toolbox for her hand tools when she was six." But since then? Nothing.

Jon hadn't seen the toolbox in years. It was probably on a dusty shelf in the basement, full of cobwebs. "When she got to playing with other girls in school, she lost interest."

"Well, the interest is back."

"Thanks. You've given me a lot to consider. Maybe she *would* be interested in learning something from her old man."

"She may surprise you and say yes." The older man chuckled. "She's at an age where girls can be hard on their parents. Try not to be disappointed if she says no the first time. But keep asking and she'll likely come around."

"Surprise me? I've just had my mind blown. What I don't get is if I didn't know this about my own daughter, what else am I in the dark about?" Between Ben joyriding and getting into fender benders and Blair having this secret interest, he'd had a long, confusing day.

Life with teens. He wondered what Trix would have to say about this turn of events.

But he'd promised himself to not unload on Trix anymore. She had enough on her mind with her baby, not having the father in the picture, and the studio renovation. She didn't need to hear his whining, too.

After his trip to the school, Jon drove along the congested town square. Dickens had a slight rush hour and a one light wait at a traffic light meant too many people were on the road. The wait at the light gave him the chance to see Trix walking out of the door to Tiny Tim's Dance Studio. She wore a jolly red scarf wrapped around her neck with the ends lifting in the breeze.

He pulled along beside her and slowed to a crawl. Lowering the passenger window, he called to her. "Hey there, pretty lady." *Oh, no. That one just popped out.* He felt heat in his cheeks.

"Hey there, handsome!" she called back with a broad smile.

"Got time for hot chocolate?" She was off caffeine, and he'd learned long ago to never mention coffee to a pregnant woman.

"I sure do!" She waggled her fingers cheerfully and veered into Dorrit's with a come-hither tilt of her head.

Trix was one of the prettiest women he'd ever met. Continually cheerful, despite the many stresses she must be feeling. Seeing her happy and inviting warmed his chest. A parking spot opened halfway down the block, and he took it. He didn't feel like a dad with troubled kids at the moment. No, he felt like a man who had a beautiful woman smiling at him and waiting to spend some time. Life seemed full of endless possibilities for him.

The feeling was heady and foreign, and he decided to enjoy it for as long as it lasted.

Chapter Ten

Not five minutes after joining Trix in the booth at the back of the diner Jon was over-sharing again. He tried not to tell her about Blair and the carpentry, but she'd asked how things had gone at the high school and off he'd gone, telling her more than he should.

"All these secrets my kids have make me wonder what else is going on with them. They've kept a lot to themselves." He ran his fingers through his hair and groaned. "And I promised myself I wouldn't dump this on you. I'm sorry."

Her beautiful hazel eyes looked more brown than green today as they filled with laughter at his expense. "No need to apologize," she snickered. "I don't mind in the least. Our talks take me out of my problems, and I appreciate that. It's easier to think about yours."

"Okay." He nodded at her blunt honesty. "I see that." He smiled back at her, happy to be of service. "If you want to unload on me, feel free. I'll listen." He may not have any advice other than on the renovation, but he'd try.

She chewed her lip. "My family's not saying this out loud, but I believe they're concerned about the baby's father."

"They hope he'll take responsibility?" Of course, Laurel and Mrs. Moore would prefer there be a father in the baby's life.

"Something like that. But what they'd love is for me to snag a new man. I'm afraid they may see you in that role."

She reached across the table. Then, she smiled gently as she cupped his hand under hers. "I'll understand if you don't want to be seen in public with me again. The more we're seen together, the more hope my family may have." She sighed and pulled her hand off his. He felt the loss.

"Are you aiming your sights at me?"

"Not at all. I planned from the start to raise this child on my own, with their support. Our friendly business relationship doesn't change anything for me. As for the baby, it'll be the two of us against the world. This baby will have a happy life."

"Babies are miracles and deserve the best."

She nodded. "Some more than others," she responded vaguely. "I've told you about being a geriatric pregnancy. I tried for years when I was married, but it was in vain." She shrugged as if her disappointment was nothing.

On the surface, it made sense to move forward. She was an established adult with love to give and this child was desperately wanted. But the guilt he'd seen in her gaze had been real. There was more to this story than Trix was saying. But with her eyes shuttered, he figured she had nothing else to say about it. And, in the end, it wasn't his business why she was determined to raise the child on her own.

Maybe she'd gone to a sperm bank after her marriage ended. She was successful and accomplished. Why not bring a child into her life when she wanted one so much, she'd pay to be inseminated?

She took a sip of her hot chocolate and got a dab of whipped cream on the tip of her nose. He touched the tip of his own to give her a hint and she blushed when she caught his meaning.

"When you blush, you look way too young to be having a baby." His breath had gone shallow at her loveliness. She was lush, smiling, and happy. What man could resist?

Laurel chose that moment to stop by the table. "Are you having dinner tonight, Jon?"

"No." He leaned against the banquette and pulled his mind to the present. "I should probably move along." He wasn't sure how to react to Trix's confession about her family sizing him up like a Christmas turkey.

"So, no plans to eat here?" Laurel's gaze was curious and kind.

Trix groaned and her eyes glared daggers at her mom. He looked back at Laurel and shook his head no.

"Good, because my mom has a huge ham in the oven, and we need more people to eat it. See you at her place in an hour. Ben will be there, too. He's called Blair already." She hustled away and slammed through the swinging door into the kitchen before he could reply.

Jon's mouth hung open in shock as he watched her scuttle away.

A strangled sound pulled his gaze to Trix. "There are days I hate my mother."

"She *is* the source of a lot of gossip in town," he said baldly. "That's part of the charm of Dorrit's; you get all the news in one fell swoop. But I never saw Laurel as meddlesome."

"Only with me." Trix's head sagged onto her fists. "I'm sure she called Gram the moment you stepped inside the diner." She jutted her chin. "And she's even got your kids involved. What'll they think?" Anger built behind her eyes. "I could kill them both for this."

"My kids?"

She blew out a breath and smiled. "How can you joke about this? They invited your children to a strange house to share a meal with a single pregnant old lady and their handsome father. Of course they'll see it as a set up."

"When it comes to his stomach, Ben doesn't care where the food comes from and with Blair it's anyone's guess how she'll react. But you've got another problem."

"What now?" She glared at him.

"I love ham."

"And scalloped potatoes?"

His mouth watered. "Melody made her scalloped potatoes with cheese on top."

She nodded. "Gram uses good, strong cheddar."

He was a goner. "I'll bring wine for everyone but you and the kids. You three can have milk."

"Be still my heart." She sighed and made a big deal of rolling her eyes. "Please don't take this the wrong way, but once this reno job is done we'll go our own ways. Agreed? We have to set the ground rules, or my family will run you to the ground."

He nodded. "You'll have your hands full with the baby and a new gallery." He swept his gaze over her belly, a look she caught.

"And you'll be busy with your next job, and, in a snap, five years will go by, and you'll be planning your first big travel adventure."

Trix got home in record time and entered a ham-scented house, furious. Normally, she and Gram raided the fridge and cleared out whatever leftovers they found. Trix enjoyed those nights. The food was eclectic with some of this and more of that. They also got to eat their favorite foods while enjoying the easy warming prep. But this? This was the worst kind of ambush.

Jon had left Dorrit's immediately to head home and shower, giving Trix plenty of time to let Gram and Mom know how much trouble they were in for meddling.

She hung her coat and scarf on a hook in the front hall, kicked off her boots and stormed into the kitchen to give her grandmother and cousin a piece of her mind. They had no right to try to force Jon into a role he didn't want. That *she* didn't want. Brenna should've put a stop to this. The hurtful betrayal would be discussed at length.

She had her mouth open and ready to blast everyone in sight when she slammed to a halt. Gram and Brenna weren't alone. Blair was here, too. At least, a teenage girl was here and since she had the same jawline and eye color of her dad, she assumed it was Blair.

"You must be Jon's daughter," Trix said through gritted teeth. She'd be polite in front of her family if it killed her. She would not give them the satisfaction of knowing they'd got under her skin.

Blair was being handed a stack of plates to take to the dining table for this impromptu Monday night dinner party. Maybe she hoped by staying on the move she could avoid conversation. Trix followed her into the dining room.

"Yes. Are you the woman he's working for? The one with the barn?"

"That's me. Trix Warden. I'm an artist—."

"I know who you are," she said. "I did an online search." She placed the plates around the table and then stepped back into the kitchen.

"I like your hair," Trix complimented in a pathetic attempt to connect as, once again, she followed the girl.

Blair tugged on the bright pink lock of hair swept over her head. Only one side of her head was shaved.

"The color is spectacular." Trix couldn't tell if her natural color was like Jon's or her mom's.

"I saw it on one of your paintings." She crossed her arms and assessed Trix, who controlled a squirm.

Trix, unsure of the girl's real meaning said, "I'll take that as a compliment."

"Don't. It's weird to paint skin this color." Her expression read as total boredom.

"Okay." This was one tough cookie and she had to hand it to Jon for coping. The bold colors in her portraits were meant to convey mood and hot pink was a happy color. It was meant for optimistic subjects.

"Blair, sweetie, can you take the cutlery and napkins out to the table?" Gram asked in her sweetest, most vague tone. She used it when she played the old lady with people who didn't appreciate how sharp she was or if she wanted to pretend ignorance of the undercurrents in the room.

She still hadn't set eyes on her duplicitous cousin, but when she did, there'd be hell to pay.

Trix had no doubt that when Jon arrived, he'd be in for a deep grilling. Gram, Laurel and Brenna may even bring in rubber hoses and a spotlight. If they tied him to a chair, Trix would have to step in. Unless she put a stop to it now.

She walked to the oven for a look. "Almost done, I hope Jon gets here in time."

"Ham keeps and scalloped potatoes should sit for a few minutes."

Jon's son had hidden out in the living room with Jett. They were talking about the process that Billie Adamson was perfecting. Jett had opened a research and development company in Dickens to help the young teen complete her research. The conversation seemed technical, so she didn't interrupt. She needed to get off her feet, anyway. She sat in Gram's recliner, then raised the footrest and settled in.

Ben was personable and chatted comfortably with Jett and smiled winningly when she introduced herself. Hard to believe a nice kid like him would take his dad's truck, get it messed up and then pretend he didn't know what had happened.

He said he was pleased to be invited to a homecooked meal. She got the impression Jon leaned heavily toward frozen meals and take-out.

Her eyes felt heavy as she relaxed into the chair, thinking that maybe Ben should dye his hair blue. Pink for girls, blue for boys...yellow or green for others...

She woke to the sound of the front door bell a few minutes later. Blair opened the door to admit her father. They shared a few murmured words that she couldn't hear. Then Jon walked into the living room and smiled down at her. Blair stood behind him with a paper bag that she presumed contained the wine he'd promised.

"You look sleepy. Did I wake you?" he asked softly.

"You look tall from down here." She struggled sideways to reach the lever to make the recliner sit upright. Jon helped with the lever and then offered both hands to her to pull her out of the chair. "Okay, this is officially embarrassing."

She took his hands and felt her body rise to a stand. Her belly met his and heat rose like a blast to her face. "Hot," she muttered. "I'm so hot."

"You're pregnant. Hot comes with the territory."

"Pregnant, you say? How the heck did this happen?" She deflected the amused affection in his gaze.

Behind him Blair grunted and pushed roughly past Trix, brushing her shoulder and sending her off balance. Jon caught her by her upper arms to steady her, but there was no need.

Anger rolled through his eyes as he glared at his daughter's retreating back.

"Blair, apologize," he said firmly.

She glanced back. "Did I brush against you? Sorry."

"I'll talk to her later," he vowed.

"Not on my account. It was an accident." She grinned. "I think that was meant for you."

Two minutes after the meal was over, Jon rose from his chair and snapped his head to the left at his daughter. "I want to speak with you on the porch."

She glared back at him. "I'll help clear the table."

"You'll speak to me now." He turned to Mrs. Moore. "Thank you for a wonderful meal. Your scalloped potatoes were delicious, and the ham brought back fond memories."

Ben patted his full stomach. "Yeah, my mom used to put cheese on the potatoes, like you did, but yours were creamier."

"Thank you, Ben." Mrs. Moore said with a gentle smile. "Blair, you helped with setting the table. You're excused from clearing it. We'll have Ben help with that."

"Sure thing," Ben said. "Happy to."

Jon left the table and headed to the front hall. Once there he opened the door for Blair and ushered her outside. "What the heck's going on with you? I've seen you sullen and moody before, but you were flat-out rude to Mrs. Warden."

"She was so phony with me, it made me sick. Telling me she liked my hair and being all friendly when I know she—." She cut off her words and stared at the veranda floor.

"She what?"

"She's after you, Dad. Can't you see it? Her whole family wants you to be with her. And she's having some guy's kid." She crossed her arms and mimicked her mother's *mom face*. Melody would laugh if she were here. But he couldn't laugh. Instead, he stared across the lawn and kept his features stiff.

He took two breaths, while his daughter glared at him. "You're judging her for being a single mom." It seemed to him, he remembered her defending some girl's decision to do exactly the same thing just months ago.

"She smiles at you. Like *really* smiles. Not just politely, but like she *like likes* you."

"Stop. This is nonsense." *And not your business*. But he didn't blame her for thinking it was. "Mrs. Warden is my client. My boss on this project. If you haven't noticed, Mrs. Moore is also your brother's boss."

"You've never been invited to dinner with other clients."

He shook his head. "Not so. Your mom and I used to have the occasional meal with clients. And sometimes, we'd entertain them at our place. Dickens is a small town and being friendly is good for business." Melody's funeral had been huge and the support he'd received had been monumental and needed. Blair wouldn't have realized it, having been swallowed up by her own grief at the time.

She frowned and bit her lip, but her tight shoulders stayed up near her ears and he relented. "Do you remember the Labor Day barbecues?"

She nodded.

"This is the same thing. A shared meal with clients. Also called networking. If you haven't noticed, Jett's a huge investor in Dickens. He could become a prospective client. I can't afford to blow people off."

Blair looked at him from below lowered brows. "Really?"

"Really," he assured his daughter.

And just like that, Jon decided to keep to himself for a while. If Jett Somers wanted to build or renovate here in Dickens, Jon would jump at the chance to work with him. For now, though, he'd ease up on the dinners with Trix. No more coffee meetings at Dorrit's either.

He frowned when he thought about how much he'd miss Trix, but Blair needed him, and she had to come first. "Would you be interested in working with me? Mr. Dillon at the high school has high praise for your work, and I have to say, I was impressed when I saw your board on the wall in the shop class the other day."

"What? Were you checking up on me at school?"

"No. Should I?"

"No!"

He shrugged. "Then you're not interested in learning more carpentry?"

She looked at him as if he'd sprouted horns and hooves. "What's the catch?"

Chapter Eleven

lack Friday—Dickens Art Studio & Market

B Through the windshield of her hatchback the almost completed barn—scratch that—the newly named Dickens Art Studio and Market rose before Trix, resplendent in a fresh coat of red paint with cream trim. She waited for Jon's arrival, wanting a private, quiet tour.

Although she hadn't seen him alone in over two weeks, Jon had become solicitous of her condition. At least, that was one of the reasons he cited for keeping her away from the construction site. He'd become convinced she shouldn't be around the noise, the sometimes-salty language, and the dust from construction.

Her family agreed with him. To keep the peace she'd stayed away. For two whole weeks, she hadn't been inside. Instead she'd finished three paintings, delivered them to *De Rigueur*, and began several more for the studio here. She wanted to open the doors with a series hanging from the rafters. She'd come up with the name Blue Mood and had used shades as light as noon sky to dark as midnight moon. She was pleased with the series and had hopes to make an impression with any clients who came out from New York.

Two weeks without talking with Jon face-to-face had been lonely. They'd become friends and being apart, while sensible, had been unduly difficult. She missed their cozy talks and wondered how his children were doing, especially Blair.

The teen had made it plain she didn't like the blossoming friendship between Jon and Trix. She was probably too young to understand that not all friendly banter led to romance. Adults could be friendly without being involved. Trix had put Blair's attitude down to grief and possessiveness over her father.

All she knew about Blair these days was that she'd joined Jon at work after school and on Saturdays. Whenever she asked how the job was going for Blair, Jon told her things were fine, but gave her few details. They'd kept their brief phone calls impersonal, and construction related.

She suspected Jon had quit confiding in her because she didn't have any parenting experience, especially with teens. She worried sometimes that she might not do a great job with her own child. But those worries were for the dead of the night, not the bright light of day.

She wouldn't speak of those concerns, because to put voice to them might strengthen them.

Jon's pickup slowed to a halt beside hers in the ten-stall parking area in front of the building. She sat in her car and watched as he rounded the front of his truck and came toward her. She lowered her window, letting the chill air inside.

His eyes searched hers. He stared as if he wanted to see something she'd hidden. It didn't make her uncomfortable but guarded because she couldn't manage her own feelings these days. She no longer trusted her face to keep her thoughts shuttered. She attempted to look serene as he approached.

"You look excited," he said, as her face betrayed her yet again.

You look scrumptious. "Thank you, I am excited. It's been a long time since I've been inside."

"The sign will be installed later today," he explained as he pointed to the sign leaning against the wall. "As I told you when we started, there are minor finishing touches to complete. I hope you're not disappointed by what I show you."

"I remember everything you told me." She'd missed him. Just seeing him; his smile and the way his eyes lit up when he looked at her. "I won't be disappointed," she promised. "I pushed hard on a ridiculous deadline."

She'd had to promise the artists a good holiday season and she'd pressured Jon. He'd taken it in stride; calm and accommodating. But honest enough to say no if it was an impossible ask.

She opened her car door, and his hand was suddenly in her line of vision, offering to help her out. Swinging her legs outside, she accepted his hand and let him tug her gently to a stand.

"Thanks." Admitting the hatchback driver's seat was snugger than it used to be was hard, but there it was: she felt wedged behind the wheel because of her swollen belly. But not for long. She'd graduated to counting the weeks before delivery now, rather than months.

It was six. Six weeks until she was due. A New Year's baby. She wondered if this would be Dickens' first baby of the new year or the last of this year. Maybe she'd be cooling her heels halfway through January. First babies were often late.

It felt like years, not weeks since she'd spent time alone with Jon. Her silly heart fluttered at the idea of stepping through the door into the studio and having him all to herself. She was certain she'd be pleased with his work.

He unlocked the door and held it open for her. As she brushed past him, the scent of his aftershave made her smile. She'd missed his scent, the heat that he gave off, the way he spoke, the way he listened.

Then she looked around the quiet building not able to take in what she saw. Then the interior erupted into a wall of sound as all the artists hurried toward her calling out. "Surprise!"

"Congratulations!"

Her family were the first to reach her. Gram, Brenna, her mom and even Jett and Marva swarmed her. She covered her mouth in shock, while her other hand reached for Jon's. He clasped it and gave her hand a light squeeze as she found her breath again.

The studio was more than ready for the artists, it was half-filled already.

She hugged her family, thanking them all for their sneaky support and then Jon leaned into her ear. "People started filling their spaces last night. We wanted it all done but couldn't quite manage."

"I'm in shock, Jon. You made good on my promise to them."

"You told them they'd have a strong season and I want you to succeed." He squeezed her hand lightly again and she squeezed back.

"Thank you for everything," she said for his ears only. Then the waterworks began, and tears ran down her cheeks.

"It's an amazing space." The feminine voice broke through the rest of the chatter and came from the hardest person to convince. Keesha, the sculptor she'd wanted the most had finally agreed to join her only a week ago. She was shy and found it difficult to talk with people, much like Faith, who worked in natural materials. The two artists had a lot in common and Trix hoped they could form a friendship.

Keesha and Trix hugged while they thanked each other. "Have you met Faith yet?"

"Our booths are directly across from each other, so yes. She's great."

After another moment of idle chatter, Keesha returned to her stall to finish unpacking.

Jon stood at Trix's back with his palms on her shoulders. She wanted to lean against him, but Blair was across the room. Jon's breath brushed her ear. "I couldn't resist surprising you."

She turned her face toward his. "I'm blown away." He'd hit the first target date she'd asked for. "I was expecting some of the artists to trickle in over the next few days, but this is incredible."

Aware of Blair, she stepped away from Jon and began a tour. The booths were in a state of disarray as the artists and crafters sorted their goods and set up their displays at the same time.

The sights and sounds and smells pulled her from one booth to the next as she took it all in. Her dream.

Her dream had come true, and she had Jon to thank. She spun and saw him near the door, listening intently to a woodworker who made handmade toys.

She wanted to walk over there, take his hand, and drag him into a shadowy corner and kiss him like he'd never been kissed. To thank him. Only that, nothing more.

Faith Jones stood in Trix's line of sight. A huge smile broke over her face as she pulled Trix into a hug. "I'm incredibly happy with my space. Thank you for pushing me to do this. I'm not great with promoting myself, but with other artists here, especially Keesha, I'll be okay."

"Yes, you will. And I'll be here all the time," she assured her. "Which reminds me, the last time I saw my office it didn't have walls." She looked toward the loft.

"You go ahead," Faith said kindly. "I think there's a surprise in there for you anyway."

"Another one?" She couldn't believe the energy, the excitement, and the joy she felt from the busy, mingling group of people. Her family members were helping unpack and set up. Jon was talking with Blair as she opened a square box.

She climbed the stairs that Jon built to the loft level and stopped halfway to look out over the bustling group. This was her dream, her future. She looked up the stairs and saw a sturdy gate at the top and drew in a surprised breath. He'd thought of everything, even a gate to keep her child safe. *Jon. Such a good man.*

She made her way to the top, opened the gate, and walked into the office he'd built for her. There, in the corner, sat a recliner next to a wooden cradle. Tears sprang up again. The recliner had a huge red and green bow across the seat. In the other corner, a three-foot fake Christmas tree stood with twinkling lights giving off a cheery golden glow.

Christmas was just around the corner, bringing all the joy of the season and after that...her baby. She drew her hand across the bottom of her personal beachball and supported the weight for a moment.

"You'll be here soon enough, little one. And we'll have our whole lives to be together."

A throat cleared behind her and she turned to find Jon watching her closely. "Do you like it?"

"I love it. Every inch of it," she said through a sigh. "You made the cradle?"

He ducked his head. "No. Actually, it was Blair. She's not a builder after all, but a woodworker. She's great at creating smaller pieces, detailed work. I told her you might need a cradle for the first few months, and she jumped on it."

"Oh! That's sweet of her." Her heart clutched at the kind gesture. "I'll go thank her right now." She moved to leave, and his hand came out to stay her. She looked up and saw a stillness in his face.

Jon wanted to kiss her.

And she wanted him to.

"I'd like—."

"Me, too," she murmured before she raised her face and set her lips to his. Their lips melded softly, sweetly and Trix warmed. Jon must have too because his arms came up around her shoulders as he held her.

She opened her lips at his gentle probe and her warmth changed to heat as she felt a flush rise from her chest into her neck. Her cheeks must be flaming.

She didn't care, didn't wonder about right and wrong, didn't think about anything but the taste of him, of Jon.

He broke the kiss and tilted his forehead to hers. His indrawn breath spoke of how the kiss affected him. She smiled inwardly and held onto the feeling of being wanted.

"I never expected to feel like this again."

"You always read my mind." He stepped back. "But I don't see where this can lead. Not with where we are in our lives."

She crashed back to reality and nodded, wanting to cry. For once, she didn't let her emotions win. Instead of tears, she gave him a wide smile. "Right. We'll be in completely different places in our lives. This baby is coming in six weeks. And then, my life won't be my own anymore." She'd be sharing it with the most important person in her world.

He smiled back at her with a nod. "That's the way it is with babies. They steal your heart and you never, ever get it back."

"Dad? Did you ask her?"

At the sound of Blair's voice, Jon spun to face his daughter. He heard Trix draw in a deep breath and let out a quiet curse.

Blair stood at the top of the stairs hands clutched over her stomach. The girl looked nervous, but not upset. From where she stood, she probably hadn't seen the embrace he'd shared with Trix. He eased his shoulders down and plastered a welcoming smile on his face.

"No, I haven't asked her. But I told her you built the cradle."

With that, Trix bustled out from behind him and launched herself at Blair. "I'm overcome by your generosity, Blair. I love it." Her voice was breaking, and he didn't need to see her face to imagine her eyes streaming with tears. Blair went stiff as Trix hugged her in thanks.

"The work is amazing. The spindles on the sides are perfect and it rocks so smoothly."

Blair's hands came up and patted Trix's back gingerly. He'd wager she hadn't had a woman hug her this tightly since Melody's funeral when his stepmom had swooped in and gathered her close.

Trix stepped back. "Now, what did you want your dad to ask me?"

"I, um, need a favor."

"Of course, anything."

Blair ducked her head. "Could I have a space for some of my work? I don't need much room."

"One of the other artists told Blair she could have a shelf to display her game boards and things, but now, since building the cradle—"

"Dad. I can ask for myself." She cleared her throat and looked steadily into Trix's face and Jon felt a swell of pride. "I need more room because I want to do more cradles and maybe some tables for lamps. Some book racks. Maybe some other stuff."

"You need a stall?" Trix swiveled her head toward Jon. He nodded.

"I can't pay yet, though." Blair claimed her attention again.

"I see." Trix crossed her arms, mimicking Blair's stance, except her arms had to rest atop her bump. "OOF! That was a big one," she said in the strangest non-sequitur he'd heard. She released her arms and then smoothed the side of her belly.

"Was that a kick?" Blair asked in an enthralled tone.

Trix nodded. "Another one." She reached for Blair's hand and brought it to rest on her bump. "Here. This baby's playing soccer."

Blair's face went red, and she gasped. "I felt it! It's a bulge that moves."

Jon couldn't tell if she was grossed out or not. He hoped she didn't say so if she was.

"That's cool," his daughter said, in wonder.

"It is cool," he agreed.

"Did you touch mom's belly?"

He nodded. "We figured you for a gold medalist in gymnastics."

She blinked and gave them both a tentative smile. "So, what about a stall for me?"

"We'll work something out," Trix assured her. "How would you feel about talking to me about your pricing, displays, expenses, and giving me a small cut of your profits?"

"Sure, I can do that."

"To start, there's a spot under the stairs that might suit you for now. I can't charge the regular rate for that space anyway. You'd do me a favor by filling it."

"I don't have much inventory ready."

"Then that space is yours. By next year, you'll be ready for a full booth."

They'd kissed. Correction, she'd kissed Jon. But he'd definitely had the I-want-to-kiss-you look on his face before she'd made her move. She wasn't sure what to think about what they'd done, and particularly about what they'd said. Neither of them could see a real future. They were adults and had had marriages before. His had been good and happy, while hers had been tension-filled and strained.

Ironic, then, that Dale had come to her that night and that she'd sympathized with him enough to let him spend the night. And that this baby would be the result. The most thrilling thing to happen to her had come about because she'd felt sorry for her ex.

Jon was a widower and she'd never felt sorry for him. For his children, yes, of course. But if she were to spend adult time with him, pity would not be the reason.

Blair had returned to the main floor to move her few things to the open space under the stairs. She'd been thrilled and Trix hoped they'd turned a corner from that prickly first meeting when Jon and his kids had been coerced into dinner at Gram's. She was still embarrassed at her family's obvious meddling that night.

She shifted the load of guilt from her shoulders onto her mother and Gram. One day, there'd be retribution. Trix just had to come up with something suitable.

As she followed Jon down the stairs, she thought about the coming weeks. Jon would move onto his next project while she'd be busier with the studio being open. She had paintings to start and finish. More artists would move in, and work would claim her as the Christmas selling season rolled into full swing. Still, there was a part of her that wanted to hold onto what they'd shared for that too-brief moment in her office.

"You had a nice family Thanksgiving yesterday?" she asked.

He turned to look at her from the bottom step. "We undercooked the turkey," he replied with a lopsided grin. "Dinner was delayed until eight p.m. but we had dessert at six so we could hang in for the rest of the meal."

"Okay, sounds like fun."

He lifted his hard hat, tousled his hair, and settled the hat again. The action never failed to send a silly thrill through her. He was one of the most handsome men she'd seen in her life. Would she ever tamp back her reaction to him? Unlikely. Jon Carpenter could crook his finger at her when they were ninety and she'd run to him.

She'd been arguing with herself over Jon Carpenter since he'd told her of his big plans for his life. The plans that would take him away from Dickens. She was a foolish woman with stupid hormones making her think ridiculous thoughts of a life with—well—never mind that. Jon had other plans. And he deserved them.

He'd raised his children, grieved for a wife gone too soon, all while building a business. If anyone deserved his freedom, it was Jon Carpenter.

"It was fun," he was saying as he sidestepped to allow her to stand with him. "Blair baked an apple pie and a lemon meringue pie. The meringue was a bit sloppy. But it tasted great. Ben got the temperature wrong for the bird, so it wasn't ready when the rest of the food was, but since the apple pie was warm from the oven, we ate it at six." He laughed. "Like wolves," he said with a grin.

"We ate dinner in front of the television at eight."

"Whatever works," she said with a happy sigh. "Our dinner was a bit more traditional." She had a thought. "Saturday is the tree lighting ceremony in the common. Are you going?"

"Probably not. The kids tell me they're too grown up for all that kids Christmas stuff and I don't see much point going on my own."

"Kids or no kids, our whole family goes. I'll be there with Gram and Mom and the whole gang. You could hang out with us if you decide to take it in."

"I'll see. I may sit at home with a beer and watch hockey. Boston's playing the Leafs and when two of the original six play, it's like they're on fire."

Chapter Twelve

Saturday December 1- Dickens Common

Jon tried one last time to get Blair or Ben to join him for the lighting ceremony, but neither of them were willing to change the plans they had for Saturday night. Blair said the ceremony was lame and she wouldn't be caught dead there. And what if her friends saw her?

He'd decided not to point out that if her friends saw her there, that meant they were in the crowd, too. Probably with their family. *The horror.* He snorted and climbed out of his truck. He'd had to park on the far side of the park where the snowman building competition was taking place right after the square was lit up. Technically he didn't think there was enough snow, but the story was that the Zamboni driver from the indoor ice rink was having the ice shavings delivered. If they didn't work for snowman building, then a huge snowball fight would break out. Win, win.

Dickens was that kind of town with those kinds of people. He loved living here. It was quaint, kind of old-fashioned in a neighbor helping neighbor kind of way, but there was comfort in the familiar. Maybe it was age talking. He wasn't the young father he used to be, the guy struggling to make ends meet with two kids and a wife who'd given up her education to have them. Now, his struggle was different.

These days, he worried over teenagers and how they kept secrets. Would Blair tell Melody about her life if she could? Or would Blair keep things to herself even if her mother was here?

Unanswerable questions swirled. He was at a loss with Blair.

By the time he arrived at the square, the crowd was milling around. Friends called to friends and people greeted him with smiles and pats on the back as he wandered, shoulders hunched into his jacket trying to pretend he wasn't looking for one very pregnant lady.

He pulled his knit cap down to cover his ears against the chill. The weather app on his phone had said to expect snow before eight p.m. He hoped it held off long enough for the crowd to get home safely.

Slipping on an ice patch, he frowned. If Trix stepped on one, she could go down hard. Her center of gravity had shifted, and her balance was off. She'd be offended at the notion because she wanted to believe that she was as surefooted as usual, but he knew better. He did not want to relive those hours after Melody had fallen.

He stepped into the hardware store and bought ice melting granules in a plastic shaker. When he spied her, he'd make sure the area around where Trix stood was covered in the pellets.

She'd hate it, but he needed to do this for her especially if more snow fell.

With renewed purpose, he scanned the crowd. Where would her family stand to get the best view? They wouldn't be at the front because that area was full of folks with kids in strollers and people who were infirm and needed walkers or wheelchairs. Mrs. Moore was in great shape, so they could stand back from the front. But they'd be close enough to see the raised dais.

As usually happened, the square was lit only by the Victorian style streetlamps. The stores and businesses around the square had shut off their lights in deference to the occasion. Once the massive pine tree was lit up, the other buildings would follow suit and the square would be almost as bright as noon.

He moved around the outer ring of people until he saw Trix and her family and friends. Mrs. Moore, Laurel, and Marva stood with Harry, Marva's smitten friend. Jett and Brenna stood with Trix a couple of feet past the others.

Jon edged his way through the back of the crowd until he stood beside Trix. A couple of seconds passed until she glanced over at him.

"Jon," she said with welcoming warmth, "I didn't think I'd see you here." She stretched to look past him. "Ben and Blair didn't come with you?"

"I'm not cool enough to be seen with. Just cool enough to drive them around and pay for stuff."

At that, she laughed.

He pulled the shaker containing the deicer out from his side. "I thought this would be a good idea." He waited a beat. "For your Gram. If she took a fall, it could be hard on her."

An arched eyebrow spoke volumes, but Jett looked over her head at him. "Good idea. Let me sprinkle some around the others."

Jon passed him the container and let Jett be the hero to the other half of their group. Gram, Marva, and Laurel looked over at him with greetings and thanks as they waved in welcome.

Trix's nose looked pink from the cold, and she gave a shiver. He wanted, badly, to wrap her in a side hug and hold her close to share his warmth. *An automatic male response to a chilled woman. It was nothing more than that.*

He had an idea that might help with the cold. "I'll get some hot chocolate from Dorrit's table. They set up a serving stand in front of the diner."

She smiled up at him, her eyes shining with anticipation. "I'd love that."

He offered hot drinks to the rest of the group and when they all said yes, it was clear he'd need a helper.

"I'll come with you," Trix offered. "I should move around a bit anyway." She stamped her feet. "My toes are cold."

"Thanks. Maybe we should take off your boots so you can dip your toes in the hot chocolate." He offered her his arm. "Hold on, there are icy patches."

When Trix slipped her mittened hand into the crook of his elbow, he drew her close to his side. "Watch your step," he said.

"You'll catch me if I fall."

"Always."

Trix liked the sound of 'always' but it wasn't true. Jon wouldn't be in her life for much longer. A few finishing touches to the studio would be done and they'd say goodbye.

They made their way through the gathering family groups and stood in line for their hot drinks. Conversation around her family filled the time as they waited. After a few minutes, they were at the head of the line.

"Mint? Marshmallows?" The teen pouring the drinks held a paper cup, ready to fill.

"No one specified. We'll take plain, to be safe," she said. The server filled the lever on the urn for the first cup. Trix took two take-out trays.

Jon shuffled ahead to pay at the register and when he pulled out his wallet, he frowned. "There's cash missing," he said. "One of my kids helped themselves," he muttered angrily.

"We only take cash out here. You'll have to go inside to use a card." The older teen girl hooked a thumb toward the diner's entrance.

"I've got it, Jon. No worries." Trix slid a twenty to the girl. "Here you go."

"Thanks!" The cashier said brightly. "You're Laurel's daughter, right?"

"Right."

"Congrats on the baby. She's excited to be a grandma."

"Yes, she is." She passed one of the cardboard trays of drinks to Jon and then saw her change in the cashier's hand. "You keep it," she said and indicated the glass tip jar.

Jon had red blotches on his cheeks. But he fumed silently and shook his head. As they strolled back toward the group, he kept his voice low. "I went to the ATM after work and got some walking around money. I can't believe one of them would take cash without asking me. Or telling me they needed some. I'd have given it to them if they asked."

He had every right to be upset and disappointed. "Could it be a secret reason?" she wondered aloud. "Like a birthday gift for you or something?"

"My birthday's in May. Ben's teaching dance so he's got his own money now. He got paid today. He was proud of it and made a point of saying so." Jon's brow furrowed. "That means Blair. But she wasn't going anywhere she'd need cash tonight."

"Maybe her plans changed," she offered, but Jon shook his head. She didn't point out that Jon was already collecting payment from Ben for the mechanic's bill for his truck damage. It could be that Ben had other expenses and he'd fallen short.

"I'll figure it out when I get home," Jon said with exasperation. Then he smiled at her. "Right now is about me hanging out with a good friend."

She appreciated him trying to keep things light, but he wouldn't relax until he'd been in touch with his daughter. "Text her. Confirm where she is."

He pulled out his phone and called her. Jon stopped walking to focus on his brief conversation. When it concluded, he looked marginally happier. "There was a TV blaring in the background and a series of screams and giggles. Blair's doing what she said she was, watching a horror flick with her friends."

They heard a voice over the crowd as someone tested the microphone and speakers from the raised dais.

"Do you want to check with Ben next?"

"He said he'd be tobogganing behind Holly Hill Inn. He left his phone at home." He nodded toward where her family waited. "We'll deliver the drinks and see the lighting, then decide what's next."

"Perfect." Someone bumped her elbow as they brushed by her, and she joggled her tray of hot drinks. "We need to get back to the family."

Amid the thanks for the drinks, Jon fell to silence. He was clearly working through his disappointment with his children.

She hooked her hand into his elbow and drew him away. "Are you okay? Want to go home?"

"No point going there because neither of them is at home anyway. I won't get my answers tonight." His lips lifted at the corners. "I'm glad to be here, among friends."

"I'm happy you're here, too." He snugged her hand closer to his body and she willingly followed, enjoying the warmth he shared.

The mayor called the group to attention and the square full of people quieted. A baby giggled to their left and a father tossed the child into the air, causing a screech of delighted laughter.

"Now, see. That's the fun part," Jon said. "You have a lot of the best ahead of you."

"Babies are different from teens," she observed.

"Night and day."

She looked up into his handsome, concerned face. "You'll come through this. Blair and Ben will, too."

"These days, kids can go very wrong very fast. They've already seen kids from school dropout, mess up their lives and worse."

"And what do they say about those kids?"

"Exactly what I just said. Dropouts who've messed up."

"Then they get the mistakes that were made. The bad choices. I'm sure they'll avoid them. Gram says Ben is a great kid; kind, considerate, and dedicated to his classes. And I don't have to tell you how talented Blair is. She's on a good path." She'd already sold at least two game boards at her tiny stall. It wasn't nearly as much as was taken from Jon though.

"The truck didn't get damaged while I was driving it. And that cash didn't disintegrate by magic in my wallet." His lips turned down at the corners. His children were testing his limits. She wondered if both were messing up or if it was one of them. If so, did the other know?

"I'm an only child so I never had another kid in the house. But my cousins covered for each other. Brenna used to forge her mom's signature if Kayley wanted to skip classes."

"They must've been a terrible influence on you," he teased.

"Sort of. I envied them their closeness and their secrets, sometimes. But they included me in lots of fun mischief, too. Regular teen stuff. I'm sure that's all you're dealing with."

"I hope so. That, I can handle."

The mayor had continued talking but Trix had tuned him out to listen to Jon, so they were taken by surprise when the huge tree was suddenly aglow with thousands of colorful lights. The square was awash in a golden hue.

Seconds later, the darkened storefronts and large homes filled with businesses on the square lit up and the crowd cheered.

Tradition was that when the lights came on, people kissed the one they were with like at midnight on New Year's Eve. Trix raised on her tiptoes and offered her lips for a quick buss.

Jon took them, pressing his rapidly warming lips to hers. "You taste sweet as Christmas pudding," he said against her mouth. Then he took another kiss and coaxed her close. Wrapped up in him, she felt the kiss change to more than a quick, celebratory peck. She reveled in the feeling. Warmth spread through her as she became something more than an expectant mother. She became a woman again, if only for a second or two.

Tears prickled. "I've missed this," she said softly. His eyes flared as he listened to every breathy word.

Jon looked down at her, his eyes misty, telling her he understood. "Me, too."

A snowflake landed on his cheek. Several more dusted his red knit cap and the crowd oohed as the air around them filled with the fat, fluffy snow, a perfect swirl of affection and Christmas warmth filling them both.

Chapter Thirteen

From his spot on the sofa, Jon heard the familiar creak of the side door entrance into the kitchen. *Thank God she was home.* Glancing at the wall clock, he took to his feet and crossed the room to lean against the archway to the kitchen. The door opened slowly. Carefully, Blair slipped inside on tiptoe, flat palm against the door to ease it closed. Made sense she'd be extra quiet, since it was after one a.m.

He flicked on the overhead light. She startled, squared her shoulders, and turned from closing the door, a guilty look on her face. That made sense, too. The guilt soon became defiance as she glared at him. Since early childhood she hated to be caught at something.

"Curfew was an hour ago and *only* if you had a reliable ride home. Otherwise, you call me, and I come get you." That was their agreement. Saturday night meant midnight, or he came for her.

Her eyes rounded. "I had a ride."

He strode closer to see if her pupils were dilated. They were fine and relief skittered through his belly. She wasn't high and looked present in the moment. "We'll circle back to the driver," he promised.

She made a move to go around him, but he sidestepped and blocked her path. Behind him, he heard Ben arrive. He must've had a sense that Jon was waiting up for Blair.

Blair looked past Jon to her brother.

"Don't look at him," he said to forestall any hidden signals. "You're talking to me."

Blair's eyes flicked back to Jon, and something went out of her. She sagged a bit, like a surrender. "What's going on?" she asked.

"Money's missing from my wallet. Not just a few bucks, but most of it." He'd been embarrassed that Trix had paid for their drinks. He'd be sure to replace her twenty-dollar bill in the morning. He'd already stopped at the ATM on the way home. "I owe Trix for a round of hot chocolate at the tree lighting earlier."

"You went? By yourself?" Ben interjected, his tone adult and demanding. "But that was mom's favorite thing."

"You were with Trix?" Blair sputtered.

"I went with Mrs. Moore, her family and friends, Trix included. You met the friends when we had dinner over there." He sighed and rubbed his neck, seeing their questions for what they were. A condemnation. They didn't want him stepping outside their prescribed boundaries. He'd tried for two weeks to be alone. To live in that mournful place he'd been since Melody died.

But he wanted a life. He did. It was time he got more social. It was time his half-grown children accepted that he deserved to move on.

"And yes," he said gently. "It was one of your mom's favorite Christmas traditions when you were a kid." He hadn't forgotten and had relived a lot of those moments when his children were too young to drive his truck, talk back, and take money that wasn't theirs. "But this discussion isn't about how I spent *my* evening."

Blair spoke in a mumble. "I'll pay you back."

"Yes, you will." He ran his hand through his hair in agitation. He'd spent time mentally framing his response if Blair admitted to taking the cash. "I'm glad you've accepted responsibility." And then the big question. "What did you need it for?"

"Gas." The way she glanced into his eyes and then away again told him more than the single syllable. Her shoulders hunched and her body language made realization bloom.

"You're the one who's been taking my truck," he bellowed in shock. Another mumble from her. "Yes."

He was totally confused now, and he half suspected that's how she wanted him. He spun to face Ben, who looked pale. He kept his gaze glued to his sister.

Jon raised his hands in surrender before things got too heated. He tracked back to Blair.

"Talk to me, L'il Bean. Just talk." The babyhood endearment must have reminded her that once, she'd thought the sun shone out of him.

"Arrrgghhh!" She pinched her lips together, but then she relented. "I came home at midnight and heard you in the shower, and I took the truck out for a few minutes, that's all. I thought you'd go straight to bed and not notice the truck was gone. My friends promised they'd pitch in for gas, but they didn't."

Ben snorted and took an unusual interest in the ceiling. "I told you they were crappy friends, and you need to ditch them."

"Shut up," Blair growled.

Jon chose to ignore the exchange between his children. He was on the cusp of an answer. "And, what? You took the money out of my wallet to drive your friends around?"

"You weren't supposed to go to the tree lighting." She huffed. "Or treat Trix and your friends to drinks." She glared at him. "If you'd done what you always do, I'd have replaced the money first thing tomorrow. I sold two gameboards, but I took checks for them." She chewed her lip. "I have to deposit the checks before I can get the cash." Her voice went small and scared as the truth came out.

"What was I *supposed* to do tonight?" He asked, his tone hard.

"You usually fall asleep in front of the TV on Saturday nights. But you went out instead."

"You took money from my wallet after supper and expected me to sack out. Which meant you felt free to drive my truck filled with teenagers." He wondered where they went, but it couldn't be far. He hadn't noticed excessive mileage on his odometer.

But every year cars filled with kids ran off the road, or swerved into oncoming lanes, or drove off cliffs because the driver was high, or inexperienced. He shuddered every time a news report like that came in. He squeezed his eyes shut.

He frowned. He hadn't checked the odometer lately. His truck's computer system kept track of when he needed oil changes, so he rarely bothered to note his mileage until tax time.

While Jon envisioned every parent's nightmare, Blair gave a one-shouldered shrug in admission. As if it was nothing.

"But instead of sacking out, I took my truck. I went out and you had already taken the cash." His heart raced as the pieces came together.

She nodded as she stared at the floor. "Yes." The word came out breathless and childlike.

Jon scrubbed at his cheeks as a picture formed. His daughter wanted to be in with the tough girls. She'd slipped out to fill his tank before he noticed the gauge and planned to replace his cash in the morning.

"You've got new friends," he said. She was hanging out with smokers, vapers and who knew who else. Druggies? He shook his head in disbelief. When? When had she let her old friends go? What kind of father was he not to notice? He'd seen the kids that day at the mall, and he'd stupidly assumed Blair was berating them for picking up bad habits. He'd still seen her as his sweet, little girl who could do no wrong.

Her fall from grace was hard on him, too. His faith in her crashed and burned. He spun toward Ben.

"You covered for her that time the bumper got hit and fell off. You took the blame." And Ben had been paying him back for the work done. Ben couldn't say exactly how the truck got hit because he wasn't there. Were all fathers this blind?

It was Ben's turn to shrug. "Yeah." He squinted. "Yes, sir."

"Because that's what you do for a kid sister," Jon added, reminded of what Trix had said about her cousins.

Ben nodded.

"I didn't ask him to," Blair said in a sulky tone.

"Both of you take a seat." He pulled out a chair at the kitchen table and sat. "We've got a lot of talking to do. And we're starting at the beginning." First off, he wanted to understand what had become of Blair's former group of friends.

By the time the three of them hit their beds, he had the full story. At least he hoped he did.

B renna leaned over from the top bunk and hung her head down to see Trix pretending to sleep. "I can see one eye is open a slit."

Family. They could read her too well. She peeped it open wider. "Why are you here again?"

"I told you. Jett's pulling an all-nighter with his security team, and I didn't feel like sleeping alone in the B&B when I could be here, pestering you about Jon Carpenter."

Trix pulled the pillow over her head. "Go away." Although Brenna probably couldn't hear her through the feathers. "I don't want to talk about Jon," she said raising the pillow from her lower face. Her eyes remained covered.

"Well, I do." Brenna dropped to the floor and then climbed into the lower bunk to spoon Trix. Next thing she knew the pillow had been tossed across the room to land on the single bed wedged against the far wall. "It's dangerous to cover your face like that. The baby may want you fully oxygenated."

This was the room the three cousins used over their Christmas visits. It had been natural for Trix to take it when she returned to Dickens in the late summer. And it was natural that Brenna would take the top bunk. When they flipped a coin for which cousin got which bed, Brenna took the top.

"I thought when you married Jett, you'd quit staying here. And stay out of my business."

"Speaking of your business, now that the remodel is almost done, will you keep seeing Jon?"

"Doubtful. You're pushing me out of the bunk." She said over her shoulder. "I don't think the baby will like smashing into the floor. And I'll tell the poor kid it was Auntie Brenna that rearranged its nose."

"Doubtful? Really? Because Jon likes you. A lot." Her breath curled around Trix's ear, and her voice rumbled in a soothing way, like it had when they were kids.

"I'm glad you're here," Trix whispered into the dark.

"Me, too."

"Thanks for coming."

"What kind of cousin would I be to choose a thick, warm queen-sized bed over this ratty old bunkbed that has you in it?"

Trix giggled. Family. Where would she be without one?

"Back to Jon."

"He's a widower with two teenagers that'll leave the nest soon. When that happens, he plans to travel the world. Sort of fulfilling his wife's bucket list. Maybe his, too."

"This means you can't see him now?"

Trix shook her head. "It would hurt if I put the intervening time in with him and he moved on. That's not what he wants, either."

"You'll have the baby to care for. You'll be too busy to miss him."

"Right. The baby's not his and I can't expect him to take us both on. It's a lost cause. Time wasted. He said before that he wouldn't want to return to diapers and dirty faces. I can't blame him. He did it all when he was young, and he deserves his freedom once Ben and Blair move into their futures." It was the natural way of things. "He's younger than I am. Did you know?"

"No. I assumed he was close though."

Tears pricked. "We kissed at the tree lighting, and I felt like a woman in his arms." And he felt like a man. He'd said as much. "It was probably hormones, but still, I enjoyed the kiss."

"It wasn't just hormones, Trix. You like him. He likes you. I don't see why you can't give him the holiday season and part ways when the baby comes. No harm done."

"It's not up to me alone, Brenna. He's got other things happening in his life right now." A frivolous month with a single, very-pregnant woman was nowhere near what Jon should be doing right now. Blair and Ben needed their father.

The sorry thing was that Trix wondered if she needed him, too.

"Seems to me that Jon Carpenter wouldn't be a waste of time. And he's not the kind of man to waste any, either. He's learned the hard way life's too short."

"Exactly," Trix muttered.

Brenna's breath evened out and after a mumbled goodnight, Trix joined her in sleep.

Chapter Fourteen

Sunday, December 2

The next day Jon caved like an underfilled water balloon at eleven forty-five and called Trix. Why bother resisting when all he wanted was to hang out with a friend. He needed to talk to her and get her take on Ben and Blair. After he and his kids had talked deep into the night last night, he thought they'd turned a corner.

But could he be sure? They'd both kept secrets lately and had hidden some of the best parts of their lives from him.

Trix answered after the first ring. "Jon, hi! How are you? The kids?"

It warmed him to hear her concern. "We're okay. Better. But this is too long a conversation without coffee. How would lunch work for you today?"

"I'm swamped with details that need to be handled before the start of business tomorrow. But dinner would work."

"Perfect, dinner it is," he agreed. "I'll spend some time with Ben in the truck today. He needs to practice driving." He ground his teeth, but there it was. His son was old enough to drive which meant he'd be responsible for the lives of others when he was behind the wheel.

He shuddered to think of the danger Blair had put herself and others in with her self-taught driving.

The conversation turned inconsequential and when he ended the call with Trix, he texted Blair. "I'm coming home. I want you in the truck with me and Ben after lunch."

"OK!"

He took the caps and exclamation to mean she was happy. But even that was suspect.

Trix slipped into a red knit dress that had folds that draped across her baby bump. Sparkles outlined the boat neck and spread across her shoulders. "Like it?" she asked Gram.

"It's beautiful. *You're* beautiful," came the dutiful reply. Her grandmother's eyes lit up. "In my day, we had to wear large tent-like styles meant to hide our bellies, as if we were ashamed or something." She sighed and ran her fingertips lightly across the dark red mini rhinestones that brought the sparkle to the Christmas-red dress. "This is gorgeous."

"Thanks, I got it today at the outlet mall. I'll be sick of wearing it by New Year's Eve. If I make it that far." She needed something nice for the holiday season. Even if she only wore it tonight, she'd wanted it on sight.

"If you do make it that long I doubt you'll feel much like partying. You'll be close to your due date and the further along you get, the more tired you'll be."

She chewed her lip. "Do you believe this is a mistake? Hanging out with Jon this way?" She didn't want to call this a date or dating.

"Let's see. Here we have two experienced adults in a friendship. You're spending time with a nice man while waiting for the largest event in your life. He knows what to expect from you having a child, while you don't."

Trix nodded. "I've heard that there's no way to prepare yourself. I mean, not really."

Gram nodded. "You tell yourself you'll shower when they nap, but you have to do laundry instead. Then, it's time to prep a meal and you end up eating standing up. Or it's four p.m. and you realize you haven't combed your hair." The smile that wreathed her face told Trix her grandmother was speaking from experience and not just teasing her.

"But it's worth all that, right?"

"Oh, sweetie, yes. All that fades away when you sit quietly and hold your sleeping child."

She clapped her hands, bringing brisk efficiency into the mood. "Until you have a baby, you can't understand the total commitment required. You'll be exhausted from labor in the first few days, then from lack of sleep, and overwhelmed by the demands of your business."

"I'm scared I'll be bad at everything."

"Maybe some days you won't be perfect. But you'll try. Sometimes it'll be the business that gets less attention, other times it'll be your own wellbeing, but it will never be the baby."

"You think?" She worried, in her quietest moments that, somehow, she'd fail this child.

"I do. This is a hard road you're on, being alone, but millions of others have done it. And done it well. But you've got us; me and your mom. We're here and we've got you."

"Oh, Gram. When Dale and I were trying for a baby, I didn't have these doubts. We were young, still in love, and I thought we'd have our whole lives together and raise our children." But when the baby didn't happen, tension had come between them. She'd wanted to go the science route, but Dale refused to spend the money. Never in a million years would she have imagined being alone through her pregnancy and then being a single, divorced mom. The fact that this child was also Dale's was the biggest irony. "Am I right not to tell him?"

"Would it be right to destroy his new family? For what? He can't be here when he lives in Oregon. Forgive me, but he's not evil, just human and made a mistake."

"I should have turned him away that night."

"Maybe." She clasped Trix by the shoulders and looked deep into her eyes. "But a man you once loved was in pain and you offered comfort. Again, not evil, but human."

Dale's wife deserved to be happy. Marie shouldn't have to live with the knowledge that he'd slipped up and come to Trix during a devastating time. It would be selfish to interfere with their lives now. Let Dale have his happy family, his dream.

Because she had hers.

"Now, go to dinner with your friend and enjoy yourself, because soon enough, this time will be in your rear view, and you won't be able to go."

"You're right, Gram, about all of it." She smoothed on a berry-red lipstick and gave her grandmother a hug.

The doorbell rang.

"He's here," Trix said with less breath than she had a moment ago and both women headed downstairs.

Trix descended the stairs, dressed in a gorgeous red dress that clung to her curves. Something danced and sparkled from one shoulder to the other, giving her a holiday glow. Her hair was held up on each side by clips that looked like rhinestone snowflakes. She was lush, glowing, and for the next couple of hours, she'd be all his. He'd missed her these last two weeks.

"You're stunning," Jon said next to her ear as he helped her slip into her coat. He patted her shoulders before she turned to face him. Up close like this, she took his breath away. Her green hazel eyes shone in the light from the ceiling fixture. Her lips invited with a soft upturn at the corners. He flashed for a moment on how she'd tasted when they'd kissed at the lighting ceremony, and he wanted to taste her again.

She blushed and let her eyelids droop. "Thank you," she said and wrapped a huge scarf around her neck and let the long ends dangle in front of her open coat. "I can't button it closed anymore, so the scarf serves two purposes."

"Let me guess. Camouflage and warmth?"

"I've always liked smart men. Have I told you that before?"

He grinned and opened the door for her. He gave Mrs. Moore, who stood watching with a delighted smile on her face, a salute. "Don't wait up," he said.

"Just have a nice time and bring me home a loaf of bread."

"Of course," Trix called back as he followed her out the door.

"We'll have a bottle of your soft apple cider," Jon ordered thirty minutes after picking up the most radiant woman in Dickens. They'd chatted about her family, mostly. Small talk that eased them toward an easy, comfortable evening.

Trix leaned across the table. "You don't have to avoid alcohol because I am."

"I kind of do. I'm not drinking and driving with a pregnant woman in a snowstorm."

"It's not a storm. It's a flurry." But she looked pleased he put her safety first.

"Whatever. The weather app said there was a chance of white outs in the area. I'm not driving through them with my reaction time slower than it should be." He picked up the menu out of habit but didn't need to read it. "I took my kids out driving today, so I've been reminded about safe driving."

"How did that go?" she asked with genuine interest.

"Blair read the booklet put out by the Department of Transportation on defensive driving and the rules of the road." She'd been glued to the pages. "She asked lots of questions which told me she'd been clueless."

"I'm confused. When was she clueless?"

"When she was driving my truck and giving her new friends rides to parties she didn't tell me about."

Trix blinked slowly twice. She tilted her head curiously. "But she's younger than Ben and not old enough to have her learner's permit."

"She's not, but it turns out she's been driving anyway."

"*She* took your truck?" Her voice fell an octave and went hollow with surprise.

He shook his head. "Ben covered for her." He told her about the revelations he'd had when he'd waited up for Blair. "After you and I decided to have dinner tonight rather than lunch, I had the afternoon free to take Ben out for practice."

"And since Blair's been driving anyway..." she trailed off, eyebrows raised.

"I decided to impress upon her the importance of safe driving techniques." He waited while the server opened the bottle of cider and poured them each a flute. After the server left, he continued. "She can drive a straight line, but that's about it. No signals, no braking skills. She drives slowly, but that could've been because I was there." He'd lost a good ten years in the twenty minutes he let her get behind the wheel.

"Ah," she said with a nod. "I see why you've sprouted several new gray hairs."

"And they're just the ones that didn't fall out from fright."

"Where were you?"

"The high school parking lot. It's dead quiet there on a Sunday."

"You're a brave man."

"Melody would've killed me for letting her drive, but she needs to avoid developing bad habits. Like the way she doesn't apply the brakes in time to stop." He shook his head. "Am I doing the right thing?"

Trix shrugged. "By teaching her, you mean. I think it shows that you love her and have forgiven her for her disappointing behavior. Do you think she'll do it again?"

He shook his head. "I trust that she's done with these friends of hers who only used her to get rides. I didn't notice when her old friends drifted away, and she took up with this new bunch. She's calling her other friends tonight. She's grounded, but I told her she could reach out."

She nodded. "Good idea. Girls need their friends, as long as they're the right ones."

"These last few weeks have been eye-opening. We talked about where I'll be in five years. I'm pretty sure it'll be in a coma."

Trix chuckled but he was serious. "I've been dealing with my own grief and blind to what my daughter's been going through. At some point, Blair moved on from one set of friends to another." He was a failure as a parent and Melody would be ashamed of him.

Jon's eyes looked wild and Trix reached across the table and searched his face, wanting to put all the sympathy she had into his heart. "You'll survive. Our parents did."

"Your mom lost her husband young, and you made it without a father."

She nodded.

If Jon could doubt his parenting, what hope was there for her? She faced raising this child alone. But her Gram's voice broke through reminding her that she was in Dickens, and she wouldn't be alone. She'd have two experienced mothers at her back.

"Let's talk about something else," Jon suggested. "Anything but parenting. The kids and I stayed up late last night and I got an earful." He smiled. "But we made real progress and Blair didn't mind being grounded. It gave her an excuse to distance from these new friends and if she reconnects with her previous group, I'll count today as a win."

"See? There you go."

He shook his head and a corner of his mouth lifted. "At least she knows how to use her flashers and that the side mirrors move to accommodate the driver's line of sight."

"And that the rear-view mirror isn't just for checking make up?"

"That, too."

He covered her hand where it lay on his. The shared warmth was a balm and put an end to the serious conversation. But his relief was palpable.

"Let's move on to other, more fun things. There's lots of news around town at this time of year with people coming home for the holidays and tourists coming to enjoy the ambiance."

She nodded assent. "Okay, we'll move on. Gram says there's been a rush on teens asking for ballroom dance lessons. Apparently, the town wants to try an old-fashioned dance competition. Have you heard about it?"

"No. Is it similar to the talent competitions on TV?" He looked relieved to have something else to focus on. She launched into more detail.

"This is nothing like the popular shows on television. Back in the nineteen twenties and thirties, there were dance marathons with a cash prize for the last couple standing. Money was scarce so young people would enter and the marathons could go for days. People paid to watch."

"How long did they last?"

"Some went on for over a thousand hours. But town council has topped ours at twelve. Six p.m. to six a.m." She grinned. "Plus, they have to ballroom dance."

"So, kids are flocking into Tiny Tim's." At her nod, he went on, "That'll be interesting. What's the prize?"

"Cash, gift cards, and electronics. And dance classes." She chuckled. "Gram came up with that one."

"Melody and I took a few lessons so we could waltz at our wedding. I remember it was fun and focusing on the steps kept my mind off how scared I was. Facing marriage and a baby and learning a trade was a lot."

"Humans are remarkably adaptable. I remind myself every day as I cross items off my to-do list." She worried sometimes that the demands on her would steal her urge to paint, but then she'd get an inspiration and take a few moments to sketch. Those sketches were piled up, waiting for her to have time for them later.

"How would you feel about taking lessons with me so you can surprise Blair? Ben could ask her to be his partner in the competition and while they're learning, you could be, too." She wanted to dance with Jon. But he wouldn't want to hold her, a beachball on legs, and move across the floor in synch. Stupid idea. She flushed hot, embarrassed by her blurted thought.

"Can adults dance in this marathon, too?"

She nodded. "Yes. The more tickets they sell, the better. It's a nominal fee. The more the merrier. Gram mentioned that the kids seemed into it. Maybe Ben's hip hop classes have started something."

"Then teach me." His eyes bored into hers and she shifted to stem the tide of male focus. "I can't come up with a better way to reconnect with both my kids. Ben and I will share this secret surprise and Blair will have a goal to help keep her occupied and away from the losers she's been hanging out with. I'm pretty sure her so-called friends won't want to get involved in ballroom dancing. Not even for prizes."

She watched his mind whirling as he nodded. He was even more handsome when he focused inwardly. His brow furrowed and his lips firmed. She shuddered in response. How would it be to have him this focused on her?

"This could be the best Christmas for us since Melody."

She covered her mouth with her fingers to keep a happy sob inside. But Antonelli's wasn't a place for loud guffaws and high fives. No, it was the kind of restaurant where couples reached across the table to hold hands and gaze alluringly into each other's eyes.

"I'd be happy to teach you. But I'm rusty and with this beach ball between us, we may not be able to hold the position correctly." She felt heat rise in her cheeks as the position she'd love to hold with him flashed across her mind. "Did they just turn up the heat in here?"

He looked across the room to where a river rock fireplace burned cheerily. "No. The gas flame's on low." His gaze returned and then roved across her neck and shoulders. She imagined the ruby rhinestones sparkling in the firelight. "Unless you're talking about how hot your dress is?"

Her temperature rose. She must be glistening by now. "You're sweet, but you're only being kind to the bloated girl."

"Maybe, but friends need to cheer each other on, right?"

"Sure, thanks." *Friends. Great.* "When will you ask Ben about getting Blair onboard with dance classes?"

"Tonight. The sooner, the better."

"When do you want to start lessons with me?"

"Tonight. The sooner, the better."

Her stomach dropped to her toes. "Then, ah, I guess I'll skip dessert." She wanted to fan her face and giggle like a teenaged girl, but a thirty-seven-year-old pregnant divorced woman had no right overreacting.

The night had changed from friends sharing a meal to dinner and dancing. She took a long sip of cider and waved to the server that they were ready to order.

Chapter Fifteen

Jon fought the urge to crowd Trix as she unlocked the door to Tiny Tim's Dance Studio. The locked snicked open and he pushed the heavy door to save her the effort. He took advantage of their closeness and leaned in for a sniff of Trix's intriguing scent.

Soon, he'd have her in his arms. The dress she wore, her perfume, the way she'd pinned her hair up at the sides, all combined to take his interest from friendly to longing. He had a name for his feelings now. He longed for her.

He wanted her smiles, her interest, her news of the day. He wanted her touches, kisses, and body snugged against him. He wanted to sling his arm over her shoulder and stroll with her.

He wanted to dance with her in the studio and in the sheets. He longed to do all those things.

She flipped on the lights and walked to the row of hooks on the wall. He followed and helped her out of her coat. Before he released her, he lifted the hair at the nape of her neck, then caught her expression in the wall of mirrors. For a frozen moment, they shared a look hot enough to burn.

He couldn't blame wine, or beer, so he blamed her for how much he wanted her. She was temptation, desire, and the cure for loneliness rolled into one and he didn't want to come up for air. It was time to face the truth.

He was attracted to Trix the way a man is to a woman. For all the years of his marriage, he'd appreciated pretty women, funny women, smart women, but he'd only been appreciating the fairer sex. He'd never strayed from his vows. Never wanted to.

When a man had had a happy marriage, was it wrong to want another? Sure, he and Melody had given up those years when other people were experiencing life in other ways, but he'd never been sorry for the choices they made as a couple. He'd wanted to live into old age with her.

But those dreams were gone along with his wife.

"Are you sure you want to do this?" Her voice came out breathy and shallow and she was still. So still. Waiting.

She wasn't asking about dance lessons or friendship. "I want this."

"For how long?"

He snapped back to attention and to the consequences of starting something serious with a pregnant woman. "I don't know. Do you?"

She shook her head. "When I'm with you, I feel like I can take on the world. That none of my worst fears will come true."

"You have fears? I'm surprised."

She lifted her chin. "I've got a bellyful of fear. Every. Single. Day." But she leaned back against him, there in front of the coat hooks while they watched themselves in the mirror.

He set his mouth near her ear. "There's a day coming soon when all those fears will be out of your belly, and you'll be the best mom you can be. Believe me, I've seen it before." He reached around to her front and smoothed his palms down the sides of her baby bump and massaged her there. "You feel good," he murmured against her. "This is the first time I've touched you here."

Tears tracked down her cheeks. "Jon. Are we're crazy to do this?"

"No, we're not. We tried the friend thing, now it's time to be honest about what we want."

"*You* want to travel."

"*You* want to live here," he responded. She nodded at his words.

"I can't stay away from you," he admitted. "You're the first person I want to call every morning. At the end of the day, I want to say goodnight."

"I can't stay away from you, either. My heart sings when I see your name on my call display." And the kisses they'd shared still made her heart zing. "I've told myself this is hormonal, but what if it isn't?"

"What if it isn't?" he asked her right back and then turned her to face him. He set his lips gently on hers, asking, begging, for permission to press harder, to open his mouth and take hers.

Instead, she opened her mouth and pressed her tongue inside. She tasted of apple cider and pasta sauce and sweet, sweet, Trix.

He was lost and never wanted to be found if it meant ending this kiss. He snugged her close as he could. She'd grown some in the last weeks and it was a stretch. A movement at his waist surprised him and he lifted his head. "We're not the only ones in the room," he said with some humor.

"You felt that?"

"I may have pressed too hard." He pulled his hips back and out of the way to avoid any more kicks. "I want to be as close to you as possible."

She giggled, blushed a pretty pink and stepped away. "That was nice," she said of the kiss.

"It was." He sighed and accepted their moment was over. But they'd come to a similar conclusion. What they felt was mutual and whatever happened in the coming weeks, they'd be together to see it play out. His heart returned to his normal beat and a weight lifted from his shoulders. "Let's dance."

"We start with the close hold." Trix moved to stand directly in front of Jon and put her left hand atop his right shoulder. Her heart still fluttered from their kisses and mutual desire. "Put your hand on my shoulder blade."

"That's familiar," he said, putting his hand at her waist.

"Higher. I need your hand on my shoulder blade." He ran his hand from her waist to the top of her ribs. She repressed a shudder of excitement. "Not quite. Slide your fingers around the back now."

"Oh," he exclaimed. "Your shoulder blade, why didn't you say so?"

She grinned. "Worse than a child who doesn't want to be here," she said with mock severity.

"You have to admit, I'm clever at finding ways to run my hands over you."

"I admit nothing. Now, pay attention, or I won't believe you ever took ballroom dance before."

"We did, but we partnered each other in a larger class." He grinned as he held his hand up at ear level so she could place her palm in his. Her bump took up the room that would normally be between their bodies. "This baby won't kick me into tomorrow, will it?"

"Not unless you misbehave."

"Yes, teacher."

"Rumba was created in Cuba. It's lively, fun, and great exercise." When he wanted to intertwine their fingers, she corrected him and put her palm between his thumb and forefinger. "This is a light clasp."

He nodded. "There's a lot of swiveling hips in rumba if I remember correctly."

"Yes, Cuban hips. I have no idea how the baby will react to the swiveling. It might feel like a rocking canoe." She bit her lip to keep from laughing.

"Since this is mostly about me learning the steps, you can take that part easy, if you want."

"That'll be baby's choice," she said. Her hips would loosen in the next weeks in preparation for delivery, but she'd be careful not to swing too widely. "I'll be sedate rather than seductive. Sedate rumba could catch on," she said through a chuckle.

"Huh? I'm stuck on the word 'seductive.'"

"You're not pulling your punches, are you?" She noticed his palm was hotter than it had been. His eyes tightened at the corners as he pulled her closer. "No kissing," she admonished as he narrowed his focus to her mouth.

"Then stop using your feminine wiles."

"My wiles are long gone."

"I beg to differ," he said and dipped her. The swoop surprised the heck out of her and when she opened her eyes he was there, leaning over her, his eyes warm and enticing, his arms a haven. She felt safe, secure, and wanted with a capital W.

She gripped him tightly in surprise. The woman buried inside her crowed at his obvious desire.

"You're incorrigible." She hadn't seen Jon in full flirtation mode before. The man was a master. He righted her again. "There's no dipping in rumba," she said as her breath whooshed out of her.

"I could've sworn rumba involved dipping." He murmured suggestively.

She wasn't sure she was breathing. Maybe she'd passed out and this was all a dream. A sexually charged dream built on hormones, lust, and loneliness.

But no, she couldn't blame her hormones this time. This was fully on Jon and his sexy come-hither attitude.

Two hours later, Jon stood in his kitchen, back against the counter, facing a happy-looking Blair. It was wonderful to see her honest smile and see she meant it. Being at home alone tonight and being in touch with her old friends had been good for her. They'd shared a group video chat and caught up on all their news. Not that she'd tell him about it, but still, she looked relaxed and content. He hadn't seen this expression on her face in months.

"You're up for this dance marathon?" Jon asked.

Blair nodded. "Sure," she said. "Kimmie suggested it, too."

Kimmie was one of her old friends. Apparently, they'd reconciled, and Blair was back in the fold.

"You cleared the air with her?"

"Of course. I told them during our chat what's been going on with me and Kimmie said it was okay. That she understood how I could mess up, since...Mom. Then she mentioned the competition and made it sound fun."

"I'm pretty sure Ben will want to register," he said.

"I guess. But he doesn't have a girlfriend to dance with."

"True." He let her think and began to wash some pots and pans that were too big to fit into the dishwasher. She got out a towel to dry. For a couple of minutes, silence reigned as they worked together.

"This competition lasts overnight. I'll have to break curfew," she said, testing him.

He nodded. "But it'll be crowded with friends and neighbors, not troublemakers. Not like a house party gone wild."

"That's right. It'll be fun, not scary."

He passed her the last saucepan to dry. "Did you feel scared with those friends?"

She hung her head. "A bit. Sometimes. I didn't like not being in charge of myself. Not being able to trust them."

"Was that why you took the truck? You wanted an escape if you needed it."

"Maybe. At least I could get myself home if things went off the rails."

"I get it," he said, and he did. She'd been trying to be responsible while still fitting in with this new group. "Rock and a hard place."

The teen years were a minefield and these days the bombs that littered the ground could be deadly. His heart lurched at the near miss.

"Daddy. I'm so so sorry I put you through all that." Her voice broke and her shoulders shuddered.

"It's behind us, L'il Bean." He patted her shoulder and then she flew into his arms and hugged him like a life preserver. Whew! If this was the biggest scare he had from his teenaged daughter he'd consider himself a lucky man.

He couldn't wait to call Trix and tell her about it. He glanced at the clock. He'd promised to call by eleven and it was close to that now. "I'm off to bed," he said as he released Blair. "Are you good?"

"I'm good."

"Talk to Ben about ballroom dance classes. Apparently, the dance studio's filling up fast because of this marathon."

"Did you hear that from Trix?"

"At dinner earlier," he confirmed and walked out of the kitchen.

Chapter Sixteen

"Jon, you remembered to call," Trix said as she lit up inside at the sound of his deep dark voice. It was after eleven, but since he left her at her front door only an hour ago, she was still awake. The nap that had overtaken her mid-afternoon came in handy. She was tucked up in the bottom bunk, ridiculously pleased at hearing his voice. She felt like a teenager getting her first call from a boy. Silly, but true. "How did it go with Blair?"

"Great. Better than great. Her old group of girlfriends welcomed her back with open arms and they brought up the topic of the dance marathon. I didn't have to plant the seed. She was already interested."

"Wonderful. And Ben?"

"Will go along with anything to keep the peace with Blair. They'll take lessons with your grandmother together and practice at home, too. Ben was alarmed when he learned why she was taking my truck. He's watching out for her and will be happy to help surprise her. Don't doubt it."

"Okay, I'm glad." She stretched and her toes reached the end of the bed. "Gram needs to get adult furniture in this guestroom." Maybe she'd buy a bedroom suite for Christmas. With her needing more space after the baby came and with Brenna married, it didn't make sense to continue the tradition of 'all the kids' having a sleepover here through Christmas. 'The kids' were mid-thirties now and had lives of their own.

"What do you mean adult furniture?"

"I'm sleeping on a lower bunk. There are two bunks and one twin bed crammed into a small room. My two cousins and I sleep in here over Christmas. We have since we were out of our cribs. I don't believe the mattresses have been replaced in all this time." The rest of year the room was used for storage. "Gram keeps her Christmas decorations in here. Once they go up for the season the room's cleaned for us kids."

"Kids?"

"Who's going to tell their grandmother not to call us kids? Not this kid."

He launched into a play-by-play of his conversation with Blair and by the end, Trix was content and happy for them. "You and I will continue to brush up on the waltz and rumba when the studio's empty," he said. "Then I'll surprise Blair with a couple of dances at the marathon. I checked and the rules state that we can change partners."

"Good. There will be breaks taken. They allow the dancers to leave the floor for fifteen minutes every couple of hours." She yawned, feeling complete joy as she looked forward to the fun of the planned surprise.

"You're tired," he said as he heard her try to stifle the yawn.

"I am. I've been falling asleep mid-afternoon for a couple of days now. I settle in on the lounger in my office and drift off. The baby settles, too, so it feels like we're napping together."

"Keep track of the time then and don't drive at that point in the day." He sounded 'concerned dad' about it, which made her grin.

"I'll say goodnight, now, Jon. And don't worry about Blair, or Ben, or my naptimes. I'll be sure to be in my office from two o'clock on. The naps are only twenty minutes, but I need them."

"Sleep well, Trix. This has been a good day."

At three p.m. the following day, Trix spoke to her baby. "I swear I didn't sleep at all last night." Her back ached from the lumpy, too-short mattress. "We're moving to the twin bed," she promised the baby. "Maybe if I can stretch out full-length you won't roll around so much. But it could be time to buy that furniture I've been considering."

The broken sleep at night could be the cause of her mid-afternoon naps. "Ow, that was a good one, punkin." She shifted and rubbed the spot.

She wasn't sure when she'd begun to talk to the baby as if it was already in the room, but she enjoyed chatting. Some of the other pregnant mothers in her birth preparedness class had mentioned doing the same thing, so she figured there was nothing strange about it.

She'd had a light lunch because heavy meals took forever to digest. The Italian she'd had last night with Jon had still been around when she woke, and she hadn't wanted breakfast until late morning. Her doctor had mentioned small meals more frequently, but had she listened? No.

A soft tap on her office door alerted her to a visitor. Through the lightly etched window in the door she saw Blair. She grimaced in anticipation of what new hell the teen had in store for her. While the girl had been grateful for the space to sell her work, she'd begrudged every moment Trix had shared with Jon.

She waved Blair to come in and take a seat. "Hi, what's up?" She plastered on a welcoming face.

"My dad told me you went to dinner last night."

She nodded.

"Why?"

The stark question hung in the air while Trix processed it. "Because we enjoy spending time together." She shrugged as if the answer was self-evident and simple, but it wouldn't be easy for Blair. Still, honesty was better than covering up the truth. Blair would see through any smokescreen Trix and Jon attempted.

"But you're having someone else's kid."

"That's true."

"And you're older than him."

She nodded. "By two years, but I'm sure I don't look my best with all this—" she waved a hand in a circle over her belly— "going on. I feel bloated and fat, not to mention I waddle like a duck."

That seemed to take the wind out of Blair's sails. "Well, *yeah*. How can he want to spend time with you?" Her tone had softened from slightly demanding to fragile curiosity.

Don't mess this up. This girl's hurting. "Honestly? It's weird for me, too." She blew out a huge breath while Blair watched her closely. "Here's this great guy who's handsome and kind and worried about his kids and he likes to talk to me. Me." She widened her eyes and let her honest surprise coat her voice. "I'm as surprised as you are. But maybe he talks to me because it's safe. I don't expect anything from him. If you haven't noticed, I'm in charge of my life. With the studio taking off and my paintings selling well in a Manhattan gallery, I don't need a man to take care of me." She smiled. "You can quit wondering if I'm after him for his money."

"So you don't need a husband? You're not out to reel him in?"

She was tempted to laugh, but decided sincerity was the higher road. "No. I don't want to reel him in. The fact is, I'm established in a life I've built myself." She needed Blair to understand the difference between a pregnant teen and a geriatric pregnant woman of means. "Hey, if I was young like your mom was when she found out about your brother coming, then yes, I'd want the father's support. But that's not where I am in life. It's hard to imagine, but not every single mom needs a man. Not financially. Plus, I have my mom and grandmother to help me with the baby."

Blair frowned. "There were two girls in school last year and they both dropped out. One got married and the other ran off with her boyfriend."

Trix nodded and let the girl think.

After a moment, Trix shifted because the baby insisted on jumping on a trampoline. "I have to walk around a bit." She rose and stretched. "When the time comes, I'll be birthing a toddler. There's no way a tiny baby can kick this hard." She arched her back and took a few steps. "That's better."

"You and my dad are just friends, then."

"I see us as support for each other. He reassures me when I get scared about my mothering skills, and I'm there when he's scared that he's messing things up with you and Ben. The whole truck thing was hard for him."

Her face went blotchy. "He told you about that?"

"Yes." She waited for a protest, but when one didn't come, she explained further. "He doesn't have your mom to talk to. He's afraid of how he's handling things." She leaned her butt on the corner of her desk. Blair looked confused and Trix was reminded that children don't see their parents as vulnerable. "He's afraid he's messing you up."

"My dad's not afraid of anything," Blair said on a reverent breath, like a little girl proud of her daddy. "He's not messing me up." She chewed her lip, considering.

"He's not scared of anything in the wide world," Trix said softly. "But the thought of losing you terrifies him."

Blair's brows shot up.

Trix decided not to get into specifics about Blair's bad influences. She had to let Blair puzzle things out on her own. But the child-woman needed more pieces of the puzzle.

"Parents lose their children all the time." At Blair's startled expression, she held up her hand. "Not to death, but to drugs, partying, bad influences." She hoped she'd kept it general enough that Blair didn't feel accused of anything.

Blair's thoughts turned inward. A frown formed on her pretty face. "The pregnant girl who ran off with her boyfriend. I guess she'd be considered lost?" She tilted her head, still puzzling.

Trix nodded solemnly. "I can't imagine not knowing where my pregnant teen daughter was."

"Yeah." Blair slumped into her seat. "I'm working things out with my dad," she assured.

Trix took that to mean Blair wouldn't become one of the lost. "I'm happy to hear that. It's important."

The teen ran her hand across the shaved side of her head. "I've taken a couple of orders for gameboards. People want them for Christmas gifts. Is it okay if I pay my stall rent after I sell them? I got fifty percent upfront, but I'm short on rent money because I have to buy the wood I need to make them."

"Of course. I'll waive rent until mid-January. You'll have a handle on how things will work out for you with the stall by then." She shrugged as if it were no biggie.

"Thanks. Cool." She gave Trix a tremulous smile. "Don't worry, I won't tell the other artists about the break you're giving me."

Trix decided to push her luck to the edge. Hiding their friendship from Blair hadn't worked. Including her might smooth things over a bit. "I planned to ask your dad to help me pick out a Christmas tree for the studio since he has a truck. If he's available now, would you like to come along?" It was Sunday and she hoped Jon was enjoying a day off. She didn't have time for a whole day off. There was always more she needed to do. Suddenly, picking out a Christmas tree had jumped to the top of her list.

"Sure?" Blair responded as a question, but Trix took it as a yes. Maybe even a win. "Want me to ask him?"

"Thanks, I've got a trip to the ladies' room in my immediate future." She left Blair texting as if she were writing a novel.

When she returned to the office, Blair was wearing her coat, scarf, and hat and ready to go. Next to her, Trix felt about a hundred and twenty years old. Lumbering, tired, and drained from the hubbub of opening the studio, she couldn't believe that only a few minutes ago she'd had enough energy to suggest a trip to Gridley Meadows Farm for a tree. "Your dad's available?"

"Yes." A shadow crossed her features and Dix wondered what had brought it on.

"Great. It's important that the studio be decorated for Christmas. All the artists need the barn to look like a great place to shop for the holidays."

"Well, yeah. That's one of the reasons I came in here today. I wondered if you had plans to decorate."

"Sorry we got sidetracked," Trix said. "I didn't mean to get personal."

"It's okay. I'm glad you did. Sort of. I never thought my dad would share stuff with a stranger."

"I have one of those faces. People tell me things all the time." She pulled on her coat and scarf and slung her purse over her shoulder. "He's on the way, right?"

"Apparently, when you call, he comes running."

Trix ignored the dig and led the way downstairs. When she got to the bottom, she paused. "Hey, if I fall asleep on the way, ignore it. At this part of the day, I never know if I'll drop off or not."

"Good thing we're taking dad's truck. You sure you should be driving?"

Trix grinned. The girl had listened to her dad's safe driving lectures.

"I'd love to get a twelve-foot tree but getting it to the studio would be a problem," Trix said with some consideration. "But if I get one that's short, it will look stubby and squat in such a tall space." They were in Jon's truck; Jon, and Blair sat in front and Trix dutifully sat in the back.

"What if we got three of varying heights and then more floor space will be used and people won't expect a towering tree, they'll only see how pretty the three of them are. We could decorate them the same or each tree could have its own theme." This from Blair who'd been silent until now.

Fifteen minutes worth of silence from her while Trix and Jon had filled the truck with gossip and weather comments. But they'd turned into the driveway for Gridley Meadows Farm and decisions had to be made about the tree.

"I love, love, love, that idea," Trix announced, pouncing on the plan. "Maybe we could get some white fluffy cotton snow and a short wooden fence to surround the trees," she added, thrilled at the concept. "Do you think three of the same types of trees or different ones?"

"The same," Blair said with conviction. "Ones that have a great pine scent."

"Super idea."

"I can make the wooden fence," Blair offered.

"I'll do it," Jon said. "You need to focus on making more gameboards. They're your bread and butter." The truck rumbled over the long, rutted driveway to the farm buildings.

Trix patted Blair's shoulder and she allowed it. "Thanks for offering, but your dad's right. This selling season is too important for you not to focus on what people want to buy." It warmed her heart to have the offer from her, though. "Maybe next year, we can come up with some other fun things for decoration that you could make months ahead of time."

"Like a stepladder with an elf on it who's putting on the star," Blair suggested.

"I like angels," Jon interjected. "An angel tree-topper is best."

"Mom liked stars," Blair grumbled.

"Loved them. And every year she'd let me whine about preferring an angel."

"But we *always* had a star."

"That's right L'il Bean. Every year I let her win that argument."

Blair reached for her father's hand, and they twined their fingers on the console.

Trix's eyes stung. They all loved Melody so much and it was wonderful to hear the happy memories they shared. Their handholding was a healthy expression of support, and she was pleased that Blair and Jon enjoyed exchanges like this.

She cleared her throat so they wouldn't hear the catch in her voice. "The stepladder is a cool idea. Could you paint it red?"

"Sure. The elf will be in traditional green clothing. The red ladder will be perfect."

Jon pulled into a parking spot in front of a farmhouse festooned for the holiday. Red and green tinsel garlands looped from support post to support post across the front porch. Twinkling lights decorated all the bare-limbed shrubs in front. White lights marched around the windows and the front door, perfectly spaced and in rigid formation. The barn to the right of the house was where all the business took place. Clear sheets of heavy plastic formed walls that fronted the barn while inside she saw a cashier and helpers. A tractor pulled in with a trailer laden with tagged trees.

Customers stood waiting for their trees to be unloaded from the trailer and then loaded onto car roofs or truck beds.

"We'd best hurry. It'll be dark soon," Jon said. "I'll go get three tags and put our names on them."

"The tree rows are laid out by size. Can you manage a ten-foot tree in the truck bed?" Trix asked.

"Yes, I'll open the tailgate and strap down the trees. Blair, you find a five- or six-footer and Trix will head for the row of eights. I'll get the ten." With that he left them to grab tags from a bucket by the entrance to the barn.

"Try for narrow bottoms," Trix said when he returned and gave out the tags. "And we'll have to get three stands that hold lots of water. I assume they still sell them inside?"

Jon nodded. "They have slow-watering bags that you strap on the bottom of the tree. They hold gallons."

Trix had seen them on the bottom of trees owned and maintained by the township. Presumably they saved water and labor. "Don't they send water to the roots? These trees won't have roots."

"We can put the stand inside the bag then fill the bag."

"Okay."

Blair stood by watching the byplay between the adults. She rolled her eyes and said, "Happy hunting." She tromped off toward her row, snow crunching underfoot.

Jon hooked his hand into Trix's elbow to hold her back. "That went well."

"I don't want to say we turned a corner. But maybe we did." She'd tell him later about the conversation she'd had at the studio with Blair. "I have more to say, but for now, let's enjoy the rest of the afternoon with her."

His hand slid down to hers and then he tugged it up to meet his lips. "Thank you."

"No need to thank me. She's creative and needs an outlet. If she finds the right one, she'll be much easier on you."

Chapter Seventeen

Jon hoped what Trix said was true. If Blair committed to her love of woodworking, maybe she'd focus her energy there instead of looking for ways to aggravate him. Being back with her old girlfriends was a good start. Fifteen minutes after entering his row of trees, his phone pinged, and he tapped the screen to find a picture of a perfectly shaped Balsam Fir tree.

The text was from Blair. "I searched online, and these trees are the most fragrant."

He responded. "Did you send this to Trix?"

Trix responded with, "I love it! I see one here, too." She sent a photo.

Blair answered. "It's kind of crooked at the top."

"I'll look some more," Trix texted.

Jon decided he'd better step up his game. He couldn't fall behind and dusk was creeping across the farm. Five minutes later, he'd found the perfect ten-foot Balsam Fir. "Found one," he texted the others. "Do you like it?"

Trix suddenly stood next to the tree. She held her phone up. "It's great."

"Hi," she said with a smirk. "I thought I'd help you, but I see you don't need any help. Blair and I found a better tree in my row that was exactly right. We tagged it and I sent her to order us some hot chocolate."

"Good, I'm about to tag this one. We can let the kid on the tractor do the chopping and hauling."

"Right." She sidled up to him and put her hands around his waist. "First, I want to do this." She raised her face to his and planted a

132

smacker on his lips. "This was fun, Jon. Blair and I actually shared a few smiles when we decided we'd beaten you to the perfect trees."

"I'll do my best to let you continue to believe your lies. As far as I'm concerned, I found the best one."

She grinned and the sight of it made him kiss her again. "I'm glad we're here," he murmured into her ear.

"At the Christmas tree farm?" He heard a whole lot of happy in her voice.

"No, at this place where I can kiss you whenever the mood strikes." He chuckled. "The mood strikes far more often than you think."

"Oh."

"And it showed up about five minutes after I laid eyes on you the first time."

"You're teasing me."

He shook his head. "Scared me to death. That's why I bolted from the barn. And then, didn't I look up to see you running to the truck flagging me down." It had been an interesting few minutes of him berating himself and then immediately getting caught up in her pretty features and her green-hazel gaze.

"I remember thinking how handsome you were and how I had to get my hormones under control if we were to work on the renovations together."

"But it's not only hormones."

"No." She snuggled under his arm and looked up at him. "It's not hormones."

Half an hour after leaving the rows of trees, Trix and Blair were inside the barn full of Christmas display and decorations. They stood beside each other staring at a wall full of ornaments and tinsel strands. "If we go one red, one white, and one blue we can't go wrong,"

Trix declared. Blair had other ideas, of course, but they'd put enough time into the discussion. Also, she was hungry, and she'd missed her nap with all the activity. She checked the Santa-face wall clock. No wonder she was hungry. Lunch was hours ago, and she'd missed her late-afternoon snack.

And her back was tired. More and more lately she was running on empty. She yawned and looked at Blair who wore a frown.

"But what about my idea for each tree having decorations based on holiday movies?" Blair replied.

Oh, right. She'd suggested that on the way in the door. "It's a fun idea for another year," Trix conceded. "But we don't have time right now." She looked to Jon, who, until this point had waited patiently for the women to decide on a color scheme or theme. "Finding all the individual ornaments would be a nightmare." She was relieved to see Jon nod in agreement.

"But I could—." Blair shook her head, cutting off her words. "I won't have time to make them."

"Two artistic people with their own vision," Jon commented. "Why not take the easy way this year and get the same decorations for all three?"

Trix and Blair glared at him, a united front against boring the public.

He held up his palms. "Hear me out. If you want a different theme for each tree, we'll be wasting a ton of time making sure we have enough for each different sized tree. Do you want to have to buy more because we miscalculated for the ten-footer?" He snapped his mouth closed.

Trix shifted her shoulders as she saw the wisdom in his suggestion. She shared a look of contrition with Blair. Then they both smiled widely. She could be a sweet girl under her cloak of teenage resentment. She'd wanted to offer to make all the ornaments based on movies. Trix love the movie theme idea, just not for this year.

"Blair, your ornament idea is great."

She shook her head. "No time left, though. D'you believe they'd sell?"

"Like hotcakes. If you can find a way to make them quickly you could design ornaments from all your favorite holiday movies."

She nodded happily. "I could have them ready to sell by this time next year."

"They'd be real keepsake ornaments. Ones to be passed down from generation to generation."

Blair eyes filled with excited anticipation. "Then let's buy gold and silver bulbs and tinsel for this year and start planning earlier next year. I'll aim for September to start selling the ornaments."

"Great. That works for me," Trix agreed. "It would be fun to make Dickens Art Studio and Market a don't miss spot for the holiday season."

Jon guffawed so hard he held his belly. "Do you realize you both went from buying one tree for this year to becoming a Dickens tradition in under three hours?"

Blair looked at Trix and they shared a smile. "Of course."

"It's how we think, right?" Blair asked.

"Go big!" Trix grinned. "Now I need to get to the truck because I'm about to fall asleep on my feet."

orrit's Diner – six p.m.
"I'll have a double stack cheeseburger and fries with a Christmas mint milkshake," Ben ordered from Laurel. Ben's request was the last and the largest of the four meals ordered. Jon suspected his son was also eyeballing the lemon meringue pie on display.

"There's only one piece of your favorite pie left. You should order it now," he suggested. Ben sat on his left in the booth while Jon faced Trix and Blair across the table. Trix had mentioned being hungry and, though she'd taken a short nap on the way home from the farm, she was tired. He'd insisted on dinner for everyone before delivering the trees to the studio.

The gratitude he'd read on Trix's face had warmed him. He'd called his son and they'd met up at Dorrit's. Ben had brought his appetite and his love of lemon pie.

Ben's ears went red. "Okay," he responded sheepishly. "May I have that last piece of lemon pie?" he asked Laurel.

Trix's mom looked toward the pie case. "I'll get it now in case Mr. Piedmont sees it. He likes the apple, too. He'll be fine if he loses out on the lemon." She walked straight over and got Ben's pie and brought it to their table.

"Thanks, Mom," Trix said with a smile. "We're heading to the studio right after we eat to decorate three trees. We got them at Gridley Meadows Farm, and bought all the decorations there, too. Want to join us?"

"I'm off at seven," she said with a nod. "Want Gram to help, too?"

"The more the merrier," Jon said, with a glance at Ben and Blair. They looked surprised but pleased at the same time. They'd both loved decorating the Christmas tree with Melody and this would be familiar but different, too. He gave Trix a nod of approval that she returned. "We'll pick up some eggnog from the store on the way over."

"Great!" This from Blair who loved the stuff.

"I'll call Gram right away. She's made rumballs. We'll bring some." She walked away to give their orders to the cook in back.

"Rumballs have rum in them, right?" Blair asked Trix who sat beside her.

"Not these ones. Gram promised she'd use something to replace the rum. She did that for my sake since I'm alcohol-free for now."

Blair looked relieved.

"Okay. Mom never made them, but a couple of my friends say they're wicked good," Ben commented as he helped Laurel by taking their drinks off her tray and passing them around. "Ow! Who kicked me?" He glared at his sister.

"I'm sure every kid in the country has sneaked a rumball or two," Jon said through a chuckle.

"I sure did," Trix supplied. "The Christmas I was fourteen my mom tried a new recipe and I ended up eating way more than my share. I remember not being able to stop. They were amazing."

The teens in the booth froze and stared at her.

After the silence stretched, Trix noticed the looks. "Not that I meant to get tipsy and go outside to sing at the top of my lungs. Have I told you I can't carry a tune to save my life?"

Laurel was back with two bowls of soup for the adults. She snorted. "The neighbors teased her for months. Called it baying at the moon."

The whole table broke into gales of laughter and Jon's heart caught on the sound. His kids, laughing with Trix and making new Christmas memories. Melody would be proud. This was what she wanted for them; what she'd told him to do.

Chapter Eighteen

The happy laughter and joy continued through the decorating at the Dickens Art Studio and Market. Trix and Blair stood back from the group and supervised the placement of the large silver and gold glitter-covered bulbs. They'd draped the tinsel garlands themselves, not trusting the non-artists in the group.

"Coming back to your plan to create Christmas movie ornaments," Trix said with some caution. Artists could be fussy about other people's suggestions. She used to hate when Dale commented on her use of color. But, in the end he'd won, and she'd put away her paints and brushes. Worst years of her life.

Beside her, Blair stiffened but kept her gaze on the trees. "What about them?"

"I'd suggest some classics that play on television every year. You could do black and white for those. They'd look great on a silver tree. Or a white one. They even sell black ones now." She shuddered melodramatically.

"Cool! And the old people could buy black and white oldie stuff."

"Hey, be careful who you call old," Laurel teased. "I'd buy black and white because those old movies mean a return to my childhood."

"Exactly," Blair declared. "But I'll also do the newer oldies like movies from the eighties. But they'll be in color."

Jon shared a look with Trix. "Because we're in our golden years. Obviously, that means color."

Trix moved to open the last box containing large gold balls for the tallest tree. Her back twinged and the baby protested by kicking her into tomorrow. "Ow, no one ever told me how much pressure one tiny baby can bring to the party." She rubbed her back.

Jon leaned in and whispered, "Want me to take you up to your office for a foot rub?"

She froze. "You'd do that?"

"They help. But they're better after a long soak in a warm bath."

"I think I'd slide to the bottom and take a nap if I climbed into a warm bath." But Gram's bathroom had a pink utilitarian tub from the nineteen sixties. "There's no soaker tub at Gram's, but it sounds like heaven."

"We have one."

Her face flamed. With a quick glance around to be sure they weren't being overheard, she whispered harshly. "Don't even think about it."

"Why not? We have something that'll make you feel rested and happy. I don't see why you'd refuse."

"It's weird, that's why."

He shrugged. "Suit yourself." Then he walked around the tree with the package of bulbs she'd opened.

She followed him. "You can't seriously believe I'd come to your home and use your bathtub. Nobody does that." It was weirdly thrilling, the idea of soaking languidly in a tub in Jon's home. He could be anywhere while she was soaking; in his room, or the kitchen, or waiting right outside the door, listening to her gentle splashes as she ran a soapy cloth over her body. She could sink into the water up to her chin and stay there until she needed to add more hot water. And then she'd do it all again.

When she came back to reality, Jon was watching her with a bemused expression. "Okay, consider yourself uninvited."

"Uninvited?" Ben asked. "To what?"

"To use the soaker tub at our place," Jon said more loudly than he should have. "Trix is exhausted, her back's tired, and Mrs. Moore's tub is shallow." He shrugged as if it was no big deal to offer an intimate thing like a bath.

Ben shrugged. "You should def do that. Nobody uses it. We all have showers."

Her back seemed to react to the suggestion all by itself. Her muscles weakened, ached, and her spine fairly crackled with delight at the idea of sliding down and being supported by deep, warm water. "Only if Blair says it's okay."

"I'll go ask her."

And the unthinkable happened.

A bit shellshocked at how Blair had taken over her evening, Trix stood beside the rapidly filling tub. Steam rose and with it, the scent of lavender.

"Here's a couple of towels." She set two on the vanity. "Shampoo and conditioner are on the shelf if you want to wash your hair." She flushed. "After my mom passed away, I'd fill the tub and lie back like when I was a kid, and she was washing my hair. It helped a bit."

"Oh, Blair. That's a sweet thing to remember. I'll do that, too. Right now I want to feel weightless or as close as I can get." She wanted to drift away and feel lazy and cosseted. "I appreciate this. What you're doing here tonight."

"You've been nice when I wasn't. I owe you."

"Sure. I get it." She blew out a breath, leaned over and turned off the faucet.

"I'll leave you to it. Dad's looking for a movie to watch and I'll be in the basement with Ben. He's teaching me some ballroom dancing for the marathon."

They'd discussed the marathon on the way home after the decorating party. Neither Ben nor Blair knew that she was teaching Jon the rumba. They had another session planned for Monday night.

"It's been a long day. If I'm still in the tub in half an hour, knock on the door. I might be asleep in there." She nodded toward the beckoning water.

"Will do."

Alone at last. Trix stripped in record time and gingerly climbed into the deep tub. As she settled weak waves sloshed against her shoulders and heaven surrounded her achy, tired body. She swooped a slow hand across her bump. "Baby mine, I'll make the most of this while I can, because I've been told this kind of time will be hard to come by after you arrive." She closed her eyes and let peace wash over her frazzled nerves.

It seemed as if Blair had stopped bristling about her friendship with Jon, but fifteen-year-olds could be moody. Still, they'd turned some corners. Maybe allowing this bath was a thank you for giving Blair time to get her stall rent together, or maybe spending more time with Trix had helped.

Whatever it was, Trix appreciated the truce. On top of everything else she was dealing with, a difficult teen who wasn't even her own felt like the last straw. She tipped her head into the water and soaked it through. Blair was right, the ritual reminded her of childhood and being bathed by her mother. Comfort in the memory rolled over her.

Reaching for the shampoo, she squirted some in her palm and lathered her head. *Oh.* The only thing better would be to have Jon's strong fingers massage her scalp. She clamped that thought hard. She wasn't here to fantasize about Jon. That way lay disappointment and grief.

It would be hard enough to live without him after the baby came. His kisses and kindness would haunt her in her quiet moments. If she had any quiet moments. Maybe it would be a good thing that the baby would keep her hopping.

Now that the bulk of the work was done on the studio, it was time to focus on her painting while she could. She'd promised three more to

De Rigueur before her due date. She had sketches, but still had days of work on each painting to do.

Could she manage it all? She needed to check in with Brenna to see how the website and marketing was coming, although, she was sure Brenna had it ready. There'd been images and ideas flowing between them for weeks. And now that the building was decorated for the season, they could add more photos.

Each artist would have their own page on the site with their best work highlighted. Most of the artists had their own sites already, but it would be good to have a sampling from the Dickens Studio, too.

Her mind twisted and turned as she rinsed her hair and squeezed out the water. A twisty mind was great for keeping thoughts of Jon at bay. She finger combed a dab of conditioner through her hair and wondered at the movie he'd chosen for his evening's entertainment.

She closed her eyes and drifted on a sea of calm until she heard a light rap at the door. "Have you drowned?" Jon asked. "Blair said you wanted a thirty-minute warning and it's closer to forty."

The water had cooled considerably. "I'm draining the tub right now," she said and raised the plug. "I'll have to wait for it to drain before I can climb out. I feel like my bones are noodles and I'm not sure it's totally safe if I try to stand in swirling water."

"Want me to come in and help?"

"No. Definitely not."

"Shall I get Blair for you?"

"By the time she gets here the tub will be empty. It's not a problem."

"Okay, but if I hear anything that sounds like trouble, I'll be in there."

"Thanks." She warmed at the idea of Jon coming to her rescue. Would he kick the door in? Swoop her up in his arms, wet and naked?

The baby rolled, reminding her that she'd feel like a wet elephant seal if he picked her up. The unappealing image made her hoist her body up to stand. She grabbed the side of the tub with both hands and put her first leg over. Once she felt the floor beneath her foot, she brought the other leg over. "I'm out safely. Go back to your movie."

"I'm holding it for you. We can watch it together. Us golden oldies."

She heard the smirk in his voice. "What did you pick?"

"My favorite. 'A Christmas Story.' Do you like it?"

"I love it! And yes, I'll watch it with you."

"I really, *really* wanted to get Ben a BB gun when he was seven, but Melody said no."

"I can't imagine why," she deadpanned. Dry and squeaky clean, she dressed and then wrapped her still-damp hair in a towel. Opening the bathroom door, she found Jon leaning on the banister at the top of the stairs. His muscular arms crossed his chest and his face looked pleased to see her. The scent of popcorn wafted to her nose. "Let's get this party started."

Inside, she had her doubts about staying awake for the whole movie, but she'd give it her best shot.

Thirty minutes later, Jon tucked a throw under Trix's chin as she dozed next to him on the sofa. She'd been valiant in her effort to stay awake, but he'd seen it was a lost cause when her head had landed on his shoulder.

He picked up her slack hand and removed it from the large bowl that held their popcorn. Her breath evened out and she snuggled closer, her belly camouflaged under the throw. He used a napkin on her beautiful, long fingers, each swipe a caress.

What he wouldn't give to be allowed to scoop her up in his arms to settle her to sleep in his bed. She'd wake in the morning, find her way to the kitchen, and join his family for breakfast. The kids would smile and welcome her.

In what universe would that happen? Not the one where his moody daughter lived, that's for sure.

A few minutes later, Ben and Blair came upstairs from the basement. Their voices sounded loud as they reached the living room because Jon had lowered the volume on the television. He raised his index finger to his lips as they arrived to see a supine Trix lying on the sofa with her head on his knee. She'd made the adjustment in her sleep, and he hadn't wanted to wake her.

Blair's narrowed gaze followed the line of Trix's body. Red blotches appeared on her neck and Jon forestalled her with a whisper. "Don't wake her. She's too tired to walk to the truck and I can't carry her."

Ben nodded. "She's exhausted. Mrs. Moore has told me Trix falls asleep at the kitchen table."

"Oh," Blair said with sympathy. "She's super busy when I see her at the studio. They all have questions and requests and want time with her."

"We didn't have a plan to go for the Christmas trees, and I wondered at her timing, but when you wanted to go..." he trailed off, hoping his daughter would see Trix's innate kindness.

"She only went because I said yes?" Blair's voice came out a hushed whisper.

Jon nodded. "I believe so." She stirred on his lap, but only to reposition her legs. Even in sleep, her hands rested protectively over where the baby lay inside her. "Sometimes I think she's lonely," he mused aloud.

"She said she was a bit scared, too." Blair sighed. "About being a good mom."

"It's a lot to raise kids alone." He smiled. "But most first-time mothers feel apprehensive. Your mom did and I was no better. After the first month and Ben was still alive, we realized we had the basics covered." They'd been sleep-deprived, scared, and fiercely protective, but no longer afraid they couldn't feed, clean, and house him.

Ben shuffled his feet, clearly disinterested in baby talk. "Come on, we should get back at it. You need to learn how to let me lead."

"Why? That part's stupid. I should lead if I want," Blair grumbled as the pair headed back to the basement. Jon smiled at a memory. Melody had had the same reaction when they'd been taking lessons.

He checked the time. It was nearing eleven and sleeping beauty had had a long, exhausting day. His wasn't much lighter. He and his crew had begun a new job today and he'd been ready to call it a day when Blair had texted about tree hunting at Gridley Meadows Farm.

Trix had performed some special Christmas magic to get Blair interested in a Christmas tree hunt. Of course, he'd changed his plans for the evening.

Instead of watching his favorite Christmas movie alone, he had company. Sleeping company, but it was great to feel the weight of her head on his thigh and hear the soft, even breaths she took. He smoothed his hand down her arm from her shoulder to her elbow. "Hey, sleepyhead, it's time to wake up." He rubbed her arm again. When that didn't work, he pressed his lips to her forehead. She shivered at his touch and a sound of protest broke from her lips.

"Lemme sleep."

"I'll call Mrs. Moore so she won't worry about you."

Chapter Nineteen

Tuesday morning

Trix woke to the feel of a blanket being pulled up to cover her shoulders. "What? Oh!" She yawned. "I'm still here?"

Blair stood over her with an amused expression. "You fell asleep, and Dad couldn't wake you."

How embarrassing. She felt weighted and heavy and foggy in her mind. "What time is it?"

"After eight. You missed breakfast. We made lots of noise, too. We assumed you'd hear us and wake up naturally, but you didn't. You must've needed the sleep." A look of concern crossed her features.

"I guess. I haven't slept this well in a long time." She scrubbed her palms down her face. "I don't remember the baby rolling around at all. Usually, that wakes me a couple of times a night."

"Maybe the kid likes it here," Blair said. "I'm leaving for school and Dad's left for work already. He's working on a store at the outlet mall and they're on a tight schedule."

She fought through the fog in her brain. "I'll call for a ride." She rubbed her temples.

"Your mom's on the way." At that, a knock sounded on the front door. Blair went to answer it. "She's on the sofa, still a bit groggy."

Her mom breezed in, trailing fresh, chilly winter air, while Trix tossed off the throw and rolled off the sofa. "It's been a long time since you had to call your mommy to come get you."

"Once," she said. "I needed to call you *once*. And that was twenty years ago." Oh, sheesh, she was old. Her teens were decades, *plural*, ago. She groaned.

"As much as I'd love to hear about that adventure, I have to get to school," Blair interjected. "I'll see you later at the studio, Trix." She came over to pat Trix on the shoulder. "Yesterday was fun. Thanks for getting people together to decorate, too." With that astoundingly sweet comment hanging in the room, Blair walked out the front door.

"Did I just hear that, right?" she muttered.

"I heard it, too," her mom assured her. "She's allowing you some room in her life."

Which was great, except Jon knew as well as she did that this meshing of their lives would all be over when the baby came. With an achy crack in her heart, she wondered if Blair understood that, too.

"I get to cross off the tree hunt and the decorating from my to-do list," she said as she headed to the bathroom. When she returned to get her coat, purse, and scarf, she texted Jon thanking him for the use of his sofa and asking how she could lock the door without a key.

"Leave the kitchen door unlocked behind you. I'll lock it after lunch today."

"Will do," she responded. To Laurel, she said, "Get me home. I have a lot to do today and I'm already behind."

Her mother sighed, long and hard. "You should take last night to heart. What you need to do is slow down and quit adding more work to your days. Your body is preparing for delivery. The baby's in the last weeks and this is when they gain the most weight. You'll get progressively more tired, heavier, and your focus needs to shift to the most important thing in your life."

"Mom, I'm fine. I relaxed in the soaker tub and afterward the baby settled and let me sleep." She flushed. "Yes, I've been stressed lately because there's so much to do."

"You don't have to do it all by yourself. You saw how it was last night. All of us pitching in. I'm taking some days off and helping you. And I won't hear another word about it."

She wasn't sure what her mom could do for her, but she was grateful for her concern and caring. "Thanks, Mom." She led the way out the kitchen door and allowed her mommy to get her home safely.

By the end of the afternoon, Trix had seen her mother parry question after question from the excited crew of artists. She handled everything from ordering bathroom supplies to offering opinions on lighting the pieces in the stalls. She saw now why Laurel was such a great server at the diner. Her mom anticipated issues and people's needs and offered an answer, even if it was only, 'I'll get back to you.' People automatically trusted that she would.

She filtered out the things that Trix didn't need to deal with and handled them alone, while reserving five minutes an hour to talk about the issues she had to pass along to Trix.

"Can I hire you? Please?" Trix begged her mother at the end of the day. They'd had a lot of browsers turned buyers through the studio as word had spread about the unique pieces to be found at the Dickens Art Studio and Market. Her mom had gone from stall to stall to get copies of the sales receipts. She'd reported back that everyone was happy, even Blair.

"Jon's daughter's stall got a lot of attention," Laurel reported. "When I noticed people there, I offered to help them and sold a couple of gameboards before she arrived after school."

"And since then?"

"She set things up to allow people to watch her work her magic with the tiny pieces of wood and sold more because the boards are handcrafted. Once you see her in action, it's hard not to want something she's done. It's like buying a collector piece."

"I'm glad." And at least in the new year when she was working here with the baby in tow, she'd still see Blair. It would be a shame to lose the connection she'd found with the girl.

D ecember 15 – *Dickens Community Hall*
       Jon stood with Trix, Laurel, and Mrs. Moore as the mayor
announced the rules for the dance marathon. Brenna and her husband
Jett stood off to the side with their friends Marva and Harry.

Since he planned on dancing only a couple of dances, Jon only half
listened to the mayor's instruction. His focus was on Blair, who stood a
few yards away with Ben. Her girlfriends clustered around them.

"Blair's best friend—Kimmie, right? — has eyes for Ben," Trix
commented for his ears only.

Kimmie was a nice girl, a good influence, and Ben had known her
most of his life.

"I'll have to keep an eye on that," he responded after a moment.
Melody had worn the same expression back in the day and Jon hadn't
been able to resist the adoration for long.

Beside him Trix hummed and swayed back and forth in a gentle
rocking motion. She claimed the motion soothed the baby. While he
was looking forward to seeing the red, scrunched face, he also accepted
the arrival would change what they had between them.

Trix had made it plain she'd be too busy to continue hanging out
with him. Her fierce independence rankled because she had no idea
how much support she'd need. He could be there for her, but she felt
they had no real future.

He wasn't sure what to think. He liked her, had from the first. But
his freedom beckoned, and when his kids left him for college, he could
go anywhere, do anything. He could catch up on some of the things
he'd missed by being such a young dad.

He'd loved raising his children and would miss them when they
left, but that didn't mean he wanted to start again with a new family.
If Melody were alive, he imagined they'd keep the family home, stay in
Dickens, and enjoy regular vacations, but without her and the kids in
the house...

He and Trix had enjoyed the last couple of weeks without Blair standing in their way. She'd enjoyed the soaker tub a few more times and had shared his bed in platonic comfort. He'd loved the feel of her next to him and had woken spooning her. Desire simmered beneath the surface between them.

They'd been careful to keep their passion private and neither of his children had pressed for more details on where their relationship was going.

The four of them were in a holding pattern as they waited for Trix's baby. They held their collective breaths and talked about the gender now and again. Boy or girl or other? Whatever, they all ended by saying they wanted a healthy baby.

If he hung around after the baby came, the platonic phase of their friendship would fly out the window. He wanted her and she wanted him, but they wouldn't be a pair anymore. There would be a child to consider too. And that child would have a stake in Jon's decisions for his future. He wasn't sure he wanted the responsibility, or the ties.

Round and around he went. Wanting Trix, but also wanting his freedom. She encouraged him to consider himself and he loved that about her. All decisions made with Melody had been about what was best for the family.

For the first time in forever, he could see a time when he didn't have to think about another living soul.

A warm hand tickled his fingers, seeking comfort. He clasped Trix's hand in his and smiled down at her upturned face. She was sweetly pert and pretty. Her features were full of burgeoning life as she'd gained weight. She glowed with health and wore maternal love like a cloak. A woman at her most beautiful.

"Blair has no idea you've been practicing dancing with me." Her comment roused him from his musing and brought him back to the present.

"None. But the first dance is about to start. I'll head over there to get her while you dance with Ben. We can switch partners anytime as long as we tell the monitors."

"Great. When the music changes to a Latin beat, we'll shock them all with our slick rumba moves."

"I requested a rumba for the second song. I don't want to tire you."

"I'm fine," she protested, as usual.

"You say that all the time, but people have noticed you struggling to keep up the pace."

"I have a lot to do before D-Day and I don't want to leave anything undone."

"This is getting old. You've been overworking and now, you've added more paintings to your to-do list."

She had the grace to look guilty. "Did Blair snitch?"

He gave her a look. "She said *De Rigueur* sold the three new portraits you sent over earlier this month. And now, you'll be driven to replace them."

She bit her lip and looked contrite. "I won't stand while I paint. I'll keep a stool nearby to sit on."

"Sure you will." He snugged her close to his side. "We'd best get over to the kids. We're out of time."

A moment later, Jon held out his hand to Blair. "Surprise," he said. "This first dance is mine." She took his offered hand and laughing, gave her brother a shocked look. "You knew?"

Ben nodded and held out his hand to Trix. "May I have this dance?"

"Of course, young man," she replied seriously. But her eyes twinkled along with the shiny red stones that danced across the shoulders of her red dress.

Blair squeezed his hand. "I'll let you lead," she teased as they joined the crowd moving onto the dance floor.

Once the dancers filled the floor, the monitors walked around checking off their lists of contestants.

"You're the prettiest dancer here," he told Blair with fatherly pride.

"Thanks, but you're my dad and you're supposed to say that."

"Did you bring another pair of shoes?"

"Yes, Trix suggested it. I have another pair for when my feet hurt."

The music swelled from the speakers and Jon moved into an easy box step while Blair dutifully followed. The dancers who didn't practice became obvious as they moved awkwardly around the room. Some minor collisions occurred but soon people became a river of swirling couples as they sorted themselves.

The center of the floor was taken up by a huge Christmas tree, donated by Gridley Meadows Farm. The scent of pine perfumed the air for now.

When the waltz wound down, Jon waved at the monitor nearest to them and smoothly moved to switch partners with Ben.

The enticing rhythm of a rumba surprised the crowd and brought a lot of laughter. Hardly anyone could complete the steps with a partner. Jon held his favorite pregnant lady in his arms as they moved to the sensual fast-paced dance.

Trix balanced beautifully and her hips moved in time to the Cuban beat. Her forehead soon glistened with her exertion.

"One dance is all I ask," he said. "Then you can rest."

"One dance is all you're getting," she chuffed back. "But, oh, it feels wonderful to move like this, if only for a few moments."

"Let's dance like no one's watching," he said as he drew her close and guided her into a turn.

Trix and Jon gave the sign they were quitting the competition and left the dance floor after their rumba. She felt they'd proved whatever point they'd wanted to make. She couldn't be sure, but maybe she wanted to show the world that preggers could have fun, too. "I had fun and the whole town has seen that I rock the rumba."

"It was more like roll the rumba, because, sweetheart, that baby was rolling." He emphasized the last word.

"You think I didn't feel that? The poor baby was looking for a lifeboat with all that sloshing. There must've been waves in there." She clucked and smoothed her belly. "Poor punkin."

"Are you all right? You didn't overdo?"

"I'm fine."

"That's your usual answer, but one of these days soon, you won't be able to brush off the question."

"I've got three whole weeks." *She only had three short weeks to get everything done.* Pressure built inside her as she did her one millionth two hundred thousandth mental check on her to-do list. She suspected once labor started her life would stop and she had to—*had to*—get through her list. Or else.

She had no idea what the 'or else' would be, but there it was, an irrational fear of her due date.

"You look more flushed than usual," Jon said. "Let's find you a seat and a cold drink."

"Thanks, I'd like that," she said gamely. He was so caring. Her heart sounded a deep call like a dinner gong at the idea of them parting ways. *Three short weeks.* Suddenly her to-do list seemed less important than filling her time with Jon Carpenter.

He strolled through the crowd, returning to her, paper cups in hand. He looked at no one but her. So focused. So manly. So vital. He deserved a woman who could give him her full attention and was certainly not her. The gong in her chest sounded again.

"Here," he said, offering her drink. "It's sparkling water. Lemon."

She shuffled along the bench that sat against the wall. Borrowed from the high school gym, she suspected. "Come, sit."

He took a seat, his long thigh against hers, his arm bringing the heat. She flushed hot.

"Drink," he ordered.

"It's not the dancing that has me warm."

"No? It's heating up in here. Soon they'll have to open a door for fresh air." He scanned the crowd, obviously searching for someone. "Blair and Ben look like they're having fun. But they've switched partners. A friend of Ben's is dancing with Blair and Ben's with Kimmie. That girl is wearing her heart on her face."

"Sleeve," she corrected automatically.

"Look at her face and tell me Ben's not her heart's desire."

She looked. "You win." And she wondered how her own face looked when she gazed at Jon.

Chapter Twenty

D*ecember 20*
Trix opened the door of Gram's house to see her Uncle Reggie and Aunt Jennifer behind a stack of tinsel covered gift boxes with shiny gift bags dangling from wrists and fingers. "Every year I tell her to keep the number of boxes and bags down so we can do this in one trip from the car. But does she listen?" Uncle Reggie groused good-naturedly. "Instead, she uses me like a pack mule."

"We all understand she's a terrible wife and mother, Uncle Reggie." Trix took the top tier of boxes from him and set them behind her on the floor. "Here, this will help."

"Love you, too, my darling niece," her Aunt Jennifer teased back. "I can't wait to drop these at the tree and take a good look at you, all chubby and cute."

"Hah hah." She loved this about the holidays. Loved that her family 'got' her and tossed her humor right back at her. In the living room, Gram waited by the tree and helped the new arrivals arrange the gifts on the floor.

Brenna and Jett followed her aunt and uncle. Jett looked bemused as usual when surrounded by the James and Moore gangs. He'd had a lonely childhood in foster care and the family love and Christmas cheer was something new for him. But from the light in his eyes, it seemed to have stuck with him from last year when he'd literally swept Brenna off her feet teaching her to tango.

Brenna on the other hand, frowned at her and tilted her head to indicate they needed a private conversation.

"The only one missing is Kayley," her grandmother said from the living room. "Is she bringing her young man to meet us?"

Aunt Jennifer glanced at her husband. "She invited him the other day, but we haven't heard if he's coming or not. She's been busy with year-end work at her firm."

Brenna gave Trix a secret eye-roll.

Uh-oh.

After the new arrivals settled in the adult guestroom, Brenna took point and explained it was time to end the tradition of having 'all the kids' in the children's room. "Jett and I are in a lovely B&B along with Marva and Harry, and we reserved another room for Kayley and...her guy. As for Trix, she needs more room for that extra person she's carting around inside her. She needs the room to herself here at the house."

"To that end, Brenna and I have ordered new furniture for Trix and the baby," Jett announced. "Our Christmas gift and baby gift rolled into one," he continued with a smile and a kiss on Trix's cheek. He looked so pleased that Trix couldn't find the words to protest their generosity.

"I'm overcome," she said. "But I'll miss the lumps in the mattress that's in there now. I finally got them to conform to my belly." They all laughed and hugged her in turn. "I love how this family describes my soon-to-be-here sweet punkin. It's more than something I'm 'carting around' inside me." Trix mugged a face.

After arranging the gifts under the tree, Trix motioned to her cousin. "Brenna, come upstairs for a moment. There's some work on the website I need done. We can leave the rabble down here."

"Whoa ho! Rabble, is it?" Her uncle said. "For that, we get the eggnog first. If there's any left, you can have the dregs."

Once she and Brenna were alone in her room with the door closed, Trix faced her cousin. "Spill. What's up with Kayley?"

"She's quit her job and is moving to Dickens. It turns out her young man, as Gram calls him, is married with two kids."

Trix gasped. "No. She was happy with him. In love." She fumed for the pain caused to her sweet and caring cousin. "They were together for over six months. She was talking about moving in with him. She wanted to take things to the next level."

Brenna nodded. "Kayley loved him, Trix. And now, she can't bear to see him at work. She stormed into his office when he was in a meeting with clients and blasted him. Kayley's —"

"Impetuous," Trix broke in. "But talk about burning her bridges. That behavior will get her blackballed in the industry."

"That's why she needs to regroup here in Dickens. Once she tells the family, I'm sure Jett will find her something to do with Somers Enterprises."

"But her work in PR is specialized, right? Will Jett need her skills?"

"Let's not worry about that for now. We'll work things out. Work and finances are the least of her worries. She's devastated and needs time to heal."

"She'll get the time she needs," Trix vowed. "We'll all make certain of that."

Another round of greetings from below startled them. "It sounds like Kayley's arrived." She felt her chest tighten as she remembered her conversation around her unexpected pregnancy. "She shouldn't worry about telling the family. After my revelation earlier this year, we've learned how to handle surprising news."

"Gram's the best, isn't she?"

"I suspect she's weathered more storms than we'll ever be told about."

It took no time for the family to see that Kayley was in distress. Her eyes were red rimmed from tears and the dark circles under them spoke of lost sleep. But she took a seat in the living room with her head held high.

"Brenna already knows this, but I've quit my job and plan to move to Dickens. Trix will be vacating when she's ready and I'll be here to keep Gram company."

"What about—." Gram cut off her question. It was clear there was no longer a reason to expect Kayley's 'young man' for Christmas in Dickens.

They'd all hear Kayley's story when the time was right.

C *hristmas Eve – Dickens Art Studio and Market*
    The building had closed an hour later than usual because people kept arriving for last-minute one-of-a-kind holiday gifts. It had been a long day at the end of a long week, but Trix felt energized. She'd helped take payments, had swept the floor, and had helped artists drape dust sheets over their displays. Her mom had gone home at closing to help Gram prep Christmas Eve dinner.

"Goodnight and Merry Christmas," she called to the last of the customers. She was about to close the door and head to her office to go over the receipts for the day, when she saw Jon's truck pull into the parking lot. A light snow had started falling, and his hair sparkled with the flakes that landed on his knit cap. His broad shoulders filled out his heavy shearling jacket.

Time had grown short and soon, she'd be without his friendship and support. The thrills they both felt would fade as the weeks passed and they'd be relegated to distant memory. She loved him so much her heart was already broken.

Before he could see, she dashed a tear off her cheek. She needed to hide how hard this was for her. Every day was a day closer to Delivery Day.

One more week.

The ache in her chest grew more painful, went deeper, whenever she saw him. She'd had to quit hanging out at his place a few nights ago. She hadn't told him that her decision was basic self-preservation. She'd hidden behind a lie and told him her new furniture had been delivered and it was more comfortable.

Of course, he'd been accepting and concerned only for her comfort. She missed his spooning, missed his cozy heat under the blankets, and missed having breakfast with him and his kids.

The truth was she'd decided to wean herself off him. Cutting things off all at once would be too hard on top of adjusting to motherhood. And it was time to get Ben and Blair used to the idea that things were changing between her and Jon.

"Hi," he said as he drew closer and stepped inside. "It's starting to blow hard out there. There's a blizzard warning and we need to be quick getting you home." He dropped a kiss on her cheek and smiled into her eyes. "Happy end of selling season. I hope it was the success you hoped for."

She ushered him inside. The wind slammed into her, and she shivered as she closed the door. "All the artists were pleased."

"Blair's ecstatic. She told me she has enough profit to buy all her supplies, pay her rent on her stall ahead of time and quit asking for allowance."

Trix mugged an impressed face. "Wow, I saw that she was busy, but that's great news."

"She also promised that she'd keep up with her chores at home despite not receiving any money for doing them."

"Very mature."

"I'll be putting her allowance into a fund for college. Not for tuition but for spending money. She deserves a nest egg after working so hard. It'll be a great surprise."

Always thinking of his children, Jon was a great father. She wished she'd known her own. But her mom had nothing but wonderful things to say about him. How much he'd loved Trix, how he'd put them first. She liked to believe he was much like Jon.

How she'd gone so wrong picking a man like Dale still surprised her. She swept her hand across her baby bump, content that she'd done the right thing by not telling her ex about this child. The knowledge would only hurt Marie and the life they were trying to build after their miscarriage. *Good luck to her. With Dale, she'd need it.*

"Are you doing something similar for Ben?" she asked as she led the way toward the staircase.

Beside her, Jon grinned. He must have something great in mind for his son.

"I plan to work on a car with him. That way, he's got it when he leaves home. We start looking for a suitable one to fix up after the holiday." A deep sadness filled his gaze. "I'll need to keep busy then, so..." he trailed away, avoiding the obvious. Jon would miss seeing Trix and would need to stay occupied.

This break was looming and for her it felt like a freight train heading her way. It did not cheer her to know Jon felt similarly.

An hour after he arrived at the studio, Jon checked the snowfall. "You believe you need to get everything done tonight, but we should leave soon. Your car will have to stay here until the snow is cleared, but I can get you home in my truck."

"My family's planning a fun Christmas Eve dinner if you and the kids would like to join us."

He frowned. "We have our own traditions for tonight. Namely, prepping the dining room table for the best breakfast we can rustle up in the morning. We set our presents under the tree, watch at least two versions of A Christmas Carol, and eat take-out. We'll get out the fancy plates and serving dishes Melody inherited from her grandmother. It's a whole thing we do." He smiled gently and a trifle sadly, too. As Delivery Day drew closer, she'd noticed him pulling away.

Self-preservation was a bitter pill sometimes.

He went on. "And with your cousin Kayley still tender about the changes in her life, you and your family don't need us underfoot."

Guilt made her nod. "I should have invited you before this. Obviously, you'll have your own traditions for Christmas Eve." She sighed and leaned on him because her back ached. But she refused to tell him because he'd fuss at her, and she didn't want fuss. Not from Jon. "I've been distracted by Kayley, and I've fallen behind on things here."

"Stop. You can't do it all." His handsome lips firmed as he ran his palm up and down her arm in comfort. He raised his face to look up at the ceiling and gave a long-suffering sigh.

"That was dramatic," she said saucily.

"I can't seem to get through to you on this. Your cousin needed support and you've given it. Something's got to give and for the most part, this place is chugging along just fine."

Her belly tightened and a band of pressure made her want to sit. She groped for the back of her office chair to hold it steady while she lowered herself to sit. Once there, she still couldn't get comfortable. "My back's giving me a royal pain. I need to rest a minute before we go rushing off into a blizzard."

"Your back? How long?"

She shifted and tried to stretch it out, but there was no give in her back muscles. They'd tightened like drums. "Earlier, I felt great. Full of energy and bounce. I made some headway on things like cleaning and helping people get their stalls sorted before they left. Now, my back's acting up. It's nothing. I'm just pooped."

"You were full of energy?"

"Yes, like the battery bunny."

"Have you felt any cramps around your belly?" He was staring into her eyes as if he was about to impart the wisdom of the ages.

"You're scaring me a bit, and no, not cramps." She bit her lip as her belly muscles tightened again. "But there's a bit of tightness across here." She rubbed her lower belly to show him where. Sweat broke out on her forehead.

"Right, we're getting out of here now. Tell me when this cramp ends and the next one starts."

"Sure, but you're overreacting." She had a week left and according to most, first babies were often late.

"I've seen this before. Twice." He moved to stand beside her chair and put both hands on her shoulders. "Now, in one move, stand."

She stood.

He kicked the chair out of the way. "Now, we get down those stairs. I'll call your family after I talk with 9-1-1."

"This is not an emergency. The baby's not due until next week and I need every day I have left to get ready." She hadn't put her new crib together yet. She planned on having Uncle Reggie and Jett work on it for her tomorrow. It seemed auspicious to set it up on Christmas Day.

"Let's move. The wind's picking up. Can you hear it?"

She was too busy focusing on a wave of pain that rolled from her back into her front, sweeping her along like a tidal wave.

"Jon." She clenched her fists as she took a couple of steps. "I believe you. About labor."

"Can you make it down the stairs?"

She nodded because the wave had receded. "Let's hurry." She took her chance and moved as quickly as she could toward the top of the stairs. Once there, she clutched the top rail.

"No, I have to wait before I go down." Another, stronger wave moved through her. Her mind went to all the things she still needed to prepare for the baby. "When I get below, please come back and bring along the cradle Blair made. I'll use it at home for now."

"A Christmas baby. You're having a Christmas baby."

"If you get me out of here and to the hospital, it won't be born in a stable!" She spoke loudly because a new cramp overtook her. The stairs beckoned but she thought better of attempting them. She sat instead.

Jon dropped to sit on the top step beside her. He pulled out his phone and she heard three short beeps as he called emergency services.

"I think, scratch that, I'm sure my girlfriend's in labor. This baby's coming fast."

Then she heard some chatter from the phone and assumed there were questions because he provided answers. "They're coming one after the other. But they just started and she's moaning already. The last time, with my wife, the moaning didn't start for hours."

She was moaning. A groan, she could accept, but a belly deep moan seemed over the top. "I thought that was the wind."

He was giving their location. "We'll be upstairs in the office." More chatter. "Yes, I can do that." He nodded, his face flushed and his eyes looking a bit wild as he glanced at her. "I'll keep the line open."

He left her for a moment as he took his phone to set it on her desk. "You need to stand and then I'll get you back in the office. They'll want to bring the gurney to you."

She felt strong arms under hers as he pulled her to her feet. He was on the step below, braced in case she fell. But she wouldn't fall. Falling would hurt her baby. With determination and a fire in her heart, Trix stepped backward, away from the stairs. She grinned. "Happy, now?"

"I would be, except there's been a pile up on the highway and our ambulances are tied up for the moment." Dickens was a small town and generally two ambulances were plenty for the population.

"You mean we're on our own?" She should've paid closer attention to her birthing classes, but she'd often spent her time checking email, convinced she'd be in the hospital long before things got serious. She fought back a rising tide of fear. "I'm having my baby here? In a barn?" She needed to leave. *Right now.*

"It's not a barn, not anymore. It's a clean room with a cradle and blankets for the baby and I'm going downstairs to get a quilt from the quilter's stall."

"Yes, get one from the back," she said, thinking quickly. "Preferably one still in a plastic bag. It'll be cleaner." The power of speech deserted her as she focused on controlling the new pain.

A voice crackled from his phone. "Mrs. Warden, how are you doing?" Jon had set the phone to speaker and Trix gasped her way through the pain. "You did good to tell Jon where to find the cleanest quilt. You should be proud of yourself."

Trix grunted. "This is getting scary," she admitted. "Things are moving way too fast. Oh! This is a sharp one." She gritted her teeth and rode it out.

"You're doing great, and our people have delivered their patients to the hospital. You're next. Just hang on for a few more minutes."

When Jon returned, she reported the update to him. But something told her she didn't have those extra minutes the operator asked for.

"You need to get me on the floor and strip off my boots, pants, and undies." She had no shame for asking. Things had suddenly become earthy and real, and her focus shifted inward to the job at hand. "I'm having this baby any minute."

She'd already felt a push. With the next one, she'd have to help move her baby toward life. "I'm sorry, Jon, but our time's run out. I wanted another week with you."

Trix wanted another week? Jon wanted a lifetime. Seeing her like this, laboring to bring her child into the world was throwing everything he thought he wanted out the window. He'd been a fool to assume he could walk away from Trix and this baby. But now was not the time to tell her.

"I'm hearing moans," the dispatcher said, reminding him they had a lifeline on the phone. "Trix, are you pushing?"

"Yesss!"

"No!" Jon wasn't ready to deal with what a push meant. "I'm alone. The ambulance hasn't arrived yet."

"They're on their way, Jon. But with Trix being full-term and this being such a fast delivery, you may have to handle this. Are you up for it?"

He nodded; his vocal cords useless as his throat threatened to close with fear. He ripped open the bagged quilt he'd found downstairs and laid it folded on the floor. "This is as soft as I can make it."

"As long as it's clean," the dispatcher said. "You're both doing great," she reassured them.

Trix stood and began pulling at the waistband of her pants. "I'm undressing now," she said to anyone who could hear her. "Can I leave my top on?"

"Yes," came the disembodied voice. "Do you have a towel or anything to put under her bottom, Jon?"

"Paper towels from the supply cabinet!" With that, he ran to the cupboard against the wall and slammed open the door, ashamed he hadn't thought of this sooner. "I have a new roll, never opened," he called.

"Great, then you know where to put them. A nice, soft, stack for a landing place," the dispatcher said, her voice soothing. "And Jon if you can, wash your hands."

By the time he returned, hands and arms scrubbed, Trix had pushed a couple more times and her face had a focused, inward look he remembered from Melody's labors. *This is it.* To Trix he said, "I'm here, I'm ready as I can be. Are you?"

She burst into tears and pushed hard.

"I'm peeking now, Trix," he said and opened her knees. "I see the baby's head, sweetheart."

From below, came the sound of a vehicle arriving. "They're here," he said for his female audience. But it didn't matter, they were still too far away to deliver this child. "I'm glad we didn't lock them out."

Trix was lost in her labor, and he wondered if she realized that help was here. She pushed again and Jon followed instructions from the dispatcher in the final moment. The baby's first moment, he corrected as the new life slid into his waiting palms.

"Oh, hallelujah! The baby's here!" Just in time for the paramedics to take over.

Jon gently laid the baby on the paper towels and scooted aside to let the man and woman handle the rest.

"Jon, what is it? Can you see?" Trix asked anxiously.

"I didn't look," he said. "I didn't have time."

Another smaller, weaker voice joined in and announced its arrival and Trix burst into tears of joy.

"I did it. We did it, Jon." She looked at him, tears brimming in answer to his own. "Thank you for being here."

"Would you like to meet your son?" The paramedic asked Jon.

"It's not my son." But he wanted him to be. Somewhere, there was a father who didn't have a clue about this little guy. "Trix, you need to tell me who to call. Who's the father? It's time he was told."

She was sobbing and holding her baby. And then she told him, and his heart shattered at the knowledge.

This beautiful baby boy belonged to the man she'd married. He collapsed onto his butt, stunned and silent as they put Trix on the gurney and strapped her in. They passed him the bundled baby and asked him to carry the boy down the stairs.

At the back of the ambulance he handed his precious bundle to the woman paramedic, and she climbed into the back and gave the boy to his mother. Trix raised her head and looked at him.

"Are you coming with us?" she asked.

"I'll follow in my truck. See you soon."

Chapter Twenty-one

Christmas Day
 Jon hadn't followed in his truck, after all. He wasn't taking her calls, either. Trix fretted, unsure what his avoidance meant. It could be that it was Christmas, and he was with his kids, or it could be that revealing Dale's paternity had spooked him. But without talking to him, she had no way of knowing what direction Jon's mind had gone.

Christmas music filled the halls of Dickens County Hospital, but otherwise the place was quiet.

The baby, her *son*, her wonderful perfect *boy* rested in her arms. He'd latched as he should, he'd opened his eyes at the sound of her voice, he'd clutched at her finger with his powerful grip. Her mom and grandmother had cooed and loved on him to their hearts' content. But now, they'd gone home to eat, and have Christmas breakfast with the family. Dozens of photos had been taken of his wizened face and her happy, smiling one.

All the nurses had wandered by to see the Christmas Eve baby who'd been born in a stable. A couple of them had complimented her on Dickens Art Studio and Market. None of them asked where the daddy was. She'd come in alone and, aside from her female visitors, she was still alone.

It hurt. She hurt.

Her phone sat by her bedside, taunting her. She dare not call or text again, because she was afraid she'd beg, and she couldn't do that to herself. Or to Jon. They'd agreed to part ways and she had to live with her decision. She'd been just as much a party to their choice as Jon was.

She just hadn't imagined the suddenness of it. Turning her face toward the window, she allowed tears to track across her face to soak the pillow. But she cried quietly, not wanting to distress the baby with the wrenching sobs she wanted to let fly.

A smile lit on her mouth as it came to her that this was the first of many sacrifices she'd make for her child.

Jon couldn't wrap his head around the sacrifice Trix was forcing her ex-husband to make without his knowledge. The man had a son he would never know. He'd have no chance to love his boy, no hand in raising him.

It wasn't right.

Her texts and calls had stopped an hour ago, but he still froze whenever he went to respond.

"Your phone was blowing up and now there's nothing. Do you even know what she named the baby?" Blair asked. "And when I can go to the hospital to visit?"

"I want to see the kid, too," Ben added when he lifted his face from his new phone. He was busy setting it up and seemed jazzed about all the bells and whistles.

"Let's eat," he said, ignoring the questions. "And no, I don't know what she's naming her son." That was another thing Dale Warden wasn't included in. He frowned. Maybe Trix would change back to Moore now that she had the boy to consider. She could still sell her art as Warden, while keeping her personal name private.

He kept wondering, as he looked at his children, what he'd have done if Melody had cut him out of her life and kept her pregnancy a secret. Her parents had been strict and traditional, and she'd been afraid of telling them. But he'd gone with her and declared his feelings. What if he hadn't been there? What if they'd sent her away?

After being with Trix, after holding that joyous little guy in his arms, he couldn't wrap his head around what she'd done to that boy's father.

It wasn't right.

She had to see how unfair she was being. Maybe she already did and didn't care.

"Dad. Dad." Ben snapped his fingers in Jon's face. "Are you in there?"

"Yeah, sure. Sorry. What?"

"We're having breakfast, remember?"

"Who fried the eggs?"

"I did. Don't worry, I checked how online." He waved his new phone in the air and his happy expression broke through.

"You're dependable, son. I'm proud of you. And if I don't say it often, you should know I feel it every day."

He rose to his feet and took his seat at the dining table, set with the fancy dishes and serving bowls. "Thanks for doing all of this," he said as he looked to both of his children. "Last night was a blur."

They looked at each other, then back at him. "About that. It's weird that you're not visiting Trix or taking her calls."

"Want to come with me?" He could use a buffer.

"Yes!" They both grinned from ear to ear and Ben offered a high five.

"Pass the sausages," he said only half convinced a visit was a good idea.

Trix's phone pinged that a text had come in. Jon asked when visiting hours were.

She texted back. "It's Christmas Day. They're not strict today. Come any time."

She waited for a text back but when it didn't come, she set the sleeping baby in his portable, tiny bassinette on wheels and shuffled to the bathroom. Once there, she brushed her teeth, her hair and skimmed some color on her lips. Her mom had brought a new cherry red nightgown and robe and she smoothed the soft flannel. White snowflakes brought a bit of festive fun to the set, and she smiled at her reflection.

She was a mother now. A different person than she'd been yesterday. A thought drifted through her mind about the studio, but it didn't settle. There would be plenty of time to think about work after she got home and into a routine with her son.

A squeak alerted her that Jack had woken, and she hustled back as quickly as she could to pick him up. After breathing in a deep draft of his sweet scent, she walked him to the window to look outside. No one had told her how addicting it was to sniff a baby's head. Was it a deep secret known only to new mothers?

She now understood some of the looks the mothers in her family had exchanged when she'd blithely said she'd be ready to work after a couple of days. As if she could set Jack down and put her whole heart and mind into work. Her every breath was irrevocably tied to this brand-new human.

Her window overlooked the parking lot. Her breath caught as she watched the other man in her heart lock his truck and walk, flanked by his two children, toward the entrance to the building. Jon had brought Ben and Blair. One carried a blue Teddy Bear, the other a pink one.

Jack would love both, she was sure.

"Sweet punkin, we have visitors. Be on your best behavior. Oh, never mind that. You do you. Because I'm sure you'll be kind and sweet and caring. Like Jon," she added, wondering if the expression in his eyes when he'd held Jack for those brief seconds meant a connection. Because it had looked serious. Hope rose in her chest.

Jack's response was to make a rumble in his diaper that would need immediate attention.

When her visitors walked in, they found her attempting to swaddle her wriggly, squirmy, little man. Tears formed.

"I can't seem to wrap him up correctly." She fretted and refused to look up at the trio who stood by the door. "There's too much cloth and he's squirming."

"Here, let me," a deep, caring voice floated across the room and landed in her heart. She did look at him then and wanted to gasp.

Jon was shuttered against her. Angry or hurt or both. Confused, she let him step up beside her and expertly turn her lively son into a bundle of immovable parts. But the handling and swaddling calmed him, and his eyelids drifted closed. It seemed a poop and diaper change had tired him.

Ben and Blair approached and leaned over the spare bed.

"I'm not in a maternity suite because technically I didn't deliver in one. This room is for two patients, but it was empty. They gave it to me and Jack." She was using the other bed as a change table.

Ben and his sister cooed and smiled at the bundled baby. "May I hold him?" she asked her father.

Jon frowned in response. "That's up to Trix," he said in a flat tone and stepped back to give her room.

"I'll pass him to you," Trix said. "If you'd like you can walk him in the hall if you're careful." She lifted Jack into her arms gingerly, showing her how to support his entire body. "You need to keep his head supported," she explained. She darted a look at Jon. The conversation he had brewing in his head would be a hard one.

She'd never seen him this distant, or this cool. He was steel when she'd expected sweet warmth. At least for Jack. But it was as if he held back. A muscle in his jaw twitched and she imagined him breaking his molars.

The teens shuffled out, keeping their voices modulated as they talked about how tiny he was and how sweet he smelled. She turned to face Jon, aware that they didn't have much time.

"Your ex-husband, Trix? And you're keeping the kid's existence from him? He deserves to hear about his son."

"You don't understand," she said, desperate to see the Jon she knew and not this icy replica. "He was married when Jack was conceived. Believe me, Jack is a miracle. We tried for years until Dale couldn't take it anymore and he" —she sighed because she'd vowed never to tell this story again— "got his receptionist pregnant." The glee he'd shown her when he'd announced his intention to divorce her had nearly broken Trix, for more than one reason.

"Then, how did you end up pregnant? You were divorced, he'd moved on and got married." He raised his eyebrows as he did the math. "You slept with him when his wife was..."

When he trailed away, Trix was afraid to let him make the obvious conclusion. "No, it wasn't like that. I'd never do that." She wrung her hands aware that Ben and Blair could return at any moment. She hushed her voice. "I was at my lowest point, agonized over them having the child I'd desperately wanted, feeling as if I'd never have that joy and Dale came to my door."

"He came to pick up something he'd left behind. A pair of lucky socks, maybe? A college sweatshirt?"

Anger flared at his flip response. "His wife had lost their baby. He was devastated and he was right to say no one would understand his pain the way I would." She raised her head, straightened her shoulders, and went on. "Yes, it was wrong. Yes, I should have given him a stiff drink and let him sleep on my sofa. But I didn't. I couldn't. I was human and so was he. For one last time, we comforted each other over the loss of a child."

He frowned and something like understanding drifted across his eyes. "But that's more reason he should be told about Jack. Be a part of his life."

She shook her head. "And tell his wife what I just told you? She's due at Valentine's Day for their second chance. They're looking forward to another child. How do I have the right to destroy their family before it begins?"

He shook his head. "What you're doing is not right."

"I'm not *wrong*, either." She clutched at his sleeve desperate to make him understand. "I'm trying to be kind. Jack won't have to know about this. They live in Oregon now. Dale and I have moved on. I'm living my best life and now I have all I've dreamed of. Dale will, too, when this new baby comes."

Jon's handsome face turned darker. "I have to go. A father should know he has children. Things could have gone differently for me if I hadn't pushed Melody's parents to accept me."

They heard a slight gasp and looked to the door where Ben and Blair stood. They'd clearly heard at least Jon's last blurted confession, maybe more.

Jon stiffened and stalked woodenly toward the door and away from her. "We decided we'd part ways when this time came. I suggest we stick to the plan."

Chapter Twenty-two

New Year's Eve
"I don't feel much like dancing," Trix said as the family gathered in the hall by the front door of Gram's house. "Jack can sleep through anything, but I need quiet time."

Her family was leaving for a relatively new holiday tradition that began last year on Christmas night. They'd had an evening of dancing at Tiny Tim's Dance Studio. This year, with Jack's arrival on Christmas Eve, the dancing had been moved.

The house had been full of love, laughter, and family with many hands willing to kiss, cuddle, and change the baby. She'd hardly had a minute to think and when she did, she pined for Jon.

Jon.

He was right, they'd known this time would come, but she hadn't prepared for this devastating loss. Especially since he'd delivered her son, had been the first to hold him, to see his face.

She blinked. Half the family had already stepped out into the chill night. Her uncle had declared that it was too cold to snow. The white stuff already on the ground crunched underfoot because it was dry and shone like diamonds in the moonlight. A perfect New Year's Eve; crisp, clean, and heralding a new beginning.

Trix waved to Marva and Harry, who stood waiting on the sidewalk for the crowd to join them before climbing into vehicles for the short drive downtown. At midnight, bells all over Dickens would toll and with any luck, she'd be sound asleep and ignoring the world.

Both the real world and the imaginary one where Jon came back to her. Because he would never come back.

Not to a woman who'd done what she'd done. Jon was a wonderful father, dedicated and loving. Of course he'd assume that Dale would be just like him. But Trix had her doubts. Dale was a demanding man, with a rigid mindset and she didn't want that influence for Jack.

But she also accepted how much Dale wanted children. The pain he'd been in that night when they'd comforted each other had been real and deep. He'd been sorry, apologetic, and oddly kind as he'd left the next morning. They'd both recognized it was a one off. A goodbye.

That grieving, contrite Dale deserved the truth. If she called him to wish him a happy New Year, she could tell him about Jack and then maybe fall into a dreamless sleep where the real world couldn't intrude.

She rubbed Jack's back, as his head rested on her shoulder. His soft breath caressed the side of her neck as she walked to the phone.

Jon dropped Ben and Blair at the entrance to Tiny Tim's, but the lights were off, so he sat in the car waiting for Trix and her family to show. He planned to head home, watch the ball drop from Times Square and wait for his kids to call to get them when they were ready to come home. According to Ben, this dance night was strictly close friends and family, and it began last year. Since he taught at the studio and Blair rented a stall from Trix, they'd become close.

Maybe his friendship with Trix had helped things along, too, but that was done. Three vehicles pulled up outside the studio and several couples greeted his kids.

Time to leave. Ben and Blair had been delivered safely into the hands of a happy group and he should head home. Still, he hesitated because he hadn't seen Trix. Maybe something was wrong with Jack, and she couldn't bring him out into the biting cold.

Or she wanted some peace and quiet at home, like he did.

Ben and Blair had been to see Trix at Mrs. Moore's place and reported that Jack was thriving while she looked dog tired. He snorted. Exhaustion came with the territory.

He frowned into the dark. Not knowing why she'd stayed home was tough. Maybe Trix had the same lonely plans he did.

Couldn't hurt to drive by the Moore place to check if she were there. His heart swelled at the thought of seeing her. Not that he'd changed his mind about telling her ex about Jack, but he couldn't convince her to do the right thing by not talking to her. A thing like this needed discussion, not silence.

They'd had wonderful talks about parenting, and Trix had helped him when he'd doubted his skills. Look how far Blair had come from being a moody teenager willing to act out. She wasn't that girl anymore and that was thanks to Trix's steady, kind advice. Her caring nature.

He found it impossible to believe that a woman who could be that sweet could also deny a man knowledge of his child. But what if she were right and Dale's marriage collapsed with the news? He couldn't see any winners in that scenario.

Maybe there was some way to compromise. He gripped the steering wheel as he gunned the engine. He wanted to fly to her. To talk this through the way they'd talked about every other thing in their lives.

He pulled into Mrs. Moore's driveway five minutes later and parked behind Trix's sporty hatchback. He grinned when he saw the 'Baby on Board' sticker in the back window. She must have been smiling when she stuck it on the glass. He wondered if that small task had been on her to-do list or if it had been impromptu.

He jumped out of his truck and bounded up the three steps to the veranda. He had his hand out to ring the bell but stopped. The doorbell chime might wake the baby. Instead, he walked to the wide living room window to have a quick look inside. Through the lace curtain, he saw her.

Trix, with Jack in her arms, feet up on the coffee table as she watched television. Gently, he rapped on the glass so as not to startle her too badly. She looked up at the sound and he waved then put his hand on the window as if to touch her.

She rose and left the room and he tracked her to the front door. It creaked open slowly as she peered out into the light that spilled from the lamps on each side of the entrance. "Jon," she said simply and opened the door to him.

He stepped inside and looked at the sleeping baby in her arms. "Oh, sorry," he said as he saw Jack wasn't sleeping, but enjoying a meal. A gulping sound rose, and Jon caught his breath. "He's hungry."

"Because he's growing fast." Her eyes misted as she looked at Jack then back at him. "I didn't expect him to grow so quickly." She kept her tone hushed.

"They all do, right through their childhoods."

"I also didn't expect to love him this much."

"Nobody does. It's overwhelming." And he felt the same about her. "Trix, I want to talk. I want to make things right between us."

She backed up to give him room to remove his jacket and knit cap. He hung both on the newel post of the staircase. Then he removed his snow boots and set them on a boot tray.

"You mean you don't want us to part with hard feelings?" Her voice sounded weak and scared.

"I don't want us to part at all." He led the way into the living room and sat on the sofa, hoping she'd follow and sit beside him.

"I'm glad," she said on a gasp. She sank to the sofa and Jack squirmed. "I've disturbed him."

Jon swept a fingertip over the baby's brow. "They feel when there's tension."

"I don't feel tense." She gave him a tremulous smile. "I feel relieved. I need to tell you something." She rested her hand on his knee and he covered it with his own. "I miss you. A lot," she continued. "When you helped me deliver Jack and I saw your face, I thought we'd be together forever. It looked like love."

He opened his mouth to confirm, but she shook her head to silence him.

"No, I need to tell you more." She bit her lip. "I've been pondering what you said about a father's right to know and while I believe there are circumstances where I might deny that importance, this isn't one of those times. Dale and I made Jack. That's a fact. Dale is married to another woman who's looking forward to a life with him and their child. That's a fact. Destroying their marriage would be cruel and, in the end, pointless."

"I'm confused. What are you saying?"

"I called Dale. Wished him a happy new year and told him about Jack. I also said it was his choice what to do with the news. I'll keep my silence if Dale wants that. But I'll also allow Dale to meet Jack if that's what he wants." She shrugged. "He wasn't happy, Jon. He's scared to lose what he has in Oregon."

"I wondered about that. After I cooled off a bit, I had to trust that you know him better than anyone." He sat in silence after that, thinking about how it must be for Dale. How out of the blue this news was. How he'd go from excited anticipation for his new baby to dread of losing his new family, all on the strength of a phone call. All because nine months ago he'd been in deep, shocked grief and turned to this wonderful, caring woman. "Until now I didn't consider the threat Jack would be to Dale's marriage, the life he'd planned with his new wife. I related it all to what could have, but didn't, happen to me."

"Of course you did. We all see life through the filter of our own experience and fears. I'm glad you pushed for acceptance from Melody's parents. It must've been scary for a kid still in high school."

He nodded.

Jack's head lolled as he released his mother from his grasp. "He's finished for now. He'll wake up in a couple of hours for more," she said as she sorted her clothing.

"You're so beautiful," he said, his heart full. "I love you, Trix. I love you and I want us to be a family."

She smiled like Mona Lisa as he waited for her answer. "I love you, too. I didn't name him Jack for no reason."

He blinked. "Jack for Jackson, right?" It was a popular boy's name these days.

"Jack is also short for John with an H. Meet Johnathan Reginald Moore. Jack for short."

"I'm just Jon, no H."

She shrugged. "It's the thought that counts. Let me put him in his cradle and we can settle in together."

He loved the sound of that. Settling in with Trix was all he wanted; now, five years from now and for the rest of his life.

When the ball dropped on the new year, Jon sat with his namesake in his arms, his fiancée's head on his shoulder and his heart full of hope for a wonderful future.

Five Years Later...

"Hurry up, Jack, we'll miss the plane. Stuff that toy in your pocket and hustle," Jon pleaded. He had a stubborn one here. He grabbed his wife's hand and used the other to clasp his son's in an iron grip. The airport in Lisbon wasn't huge, but since Jack had insisted on using the washroom and locked himself in the stall for five full minutes because he was a big boy who didn't need his daddy in there with him, they were behind schedule. They had just enough time to get to their gate.

They'd been on a two-week vacation in sunny Portugal, a country Melody had wanted to see, but Christmas in Dickens beckoned, and they were headed home in time for Jack's birthday.

After they buckled themselves into their seats and Jack was playing with his action figure again, Trix reached for Jon's hand. "Ben and Blair will meet us at the airport," he said. "Luckily, their flights dovetailed with ours."

"Uncle Dale and Aunt Marie have booked a B&B for the season. The cousins need more time together and Christmas in Dickens is magical. They'll love it."

It had taken Dale a year to tell Marie the real reason he visited Dickens every three months. But, after some heartfelt discussion, and the news of another 'cousin' on the way, the adults had agreed that a friendly relationship would be best for all their children. Understanding and kindness had won out over jealousy and anger and Jon and Trix agreed that Dale was a lucky man to have a woman like Marie. She'd stretched her heart to include Jack in their lives and now, everyone was settled, and happy.

"Liam! Sophie!" Jack broke in. "We have fun. I can teach them to skate, Momma." He widened his eyes with pride. "'cause I already knows how."

"Sophie's only three, remember," Jon said quietly. "But I'm sure you'll go easy on her." Out of the corner of his mouth, he said, "I hope."

Trix laughed the laugh he loved the most. Her indulgent mom laugh. She used it liberally with Jack, with him, and with Blair and Ben who loved her as much as she loved them.

A friendly looking woman across the aisle smiled at Jack's boisterous announcement. "Where are you heading?" she asked.

"Home," Jon replied, "to the most wonderful town in all of New England. It's time for Christmas in Dickens."

The End

If you choose your books based on reviews, I hope you'll pay it forward and share your thoughts on *The Rumball Rumba*. A sentence or two on how you felt when you closed the book would be fabulous. This is my second romance set in the quintessential New England town of Dickens, which celebrates Christmas like nowhere else.

The next book in this trilogy *The Winterland Waltz* is available through Books 2 Read, a handy *FREE* service that links you to your favorite store. Tell them once where you prefer to purchase (for Apple, Kobo, Nook and more) and you will always be taken to that store, regardless of the author you purchase. This link is one and done, at no cost to you! https://books2read.com/WinterlandWaltz

If you missed Brenna and Jett's story in *The Tinsel Tango* it's here: https://books2read.com/TheTinselTango

If you prefer to browse bookstores, please request staff to order copies of the titles you'd like to read.

To learn more about upcoming releases and special deals, sign up for Bonnie's Newsy Bits[1] on my website. New subscribers are offered a free read from another series set in Last Chance Beach.

For MORE Dickens Holiday Romances check out the series page on Amazon, which lists all titles published to date. https://www.amazon.com/dp/B09NX3BQWT The authors of these lovely, holiday themed romances are not done yet. Watch for more Dickens books in 2023!

---

1.   https://landing.mailerlite.com/webforms/landing/t6w3o6

Other Romances by Bonnie Edwards

No Bake, No Rum, Rum Balls
Makes 3 dozen

Ingredients

3 cups fine crumbs vanilla wafers (use a food processor to make them fine)

½ c ground pecans

3 TBs cocoa

1 cup icing sugar (confectioner's sugar)

3 TBs light corn syrup

1/3 cup water

2 tsps. rum flavored extract

¼ cup icing sugar for coating

Directions

Mix first 7 ingredients together in a medium bowl. Put remaining icing sugar in a zip bag. Roll mixture into 1-inch balls and refrigerate. When chilled place in bag for a gentle shake to coat. Store in bag or covered container for up to a week before serving.

Enjoy! And Happy Holidays!

Don't miss out!

Visit the website below and you can sign up to receive emails whenever Bonnie Edwards publishes a new book. There's no charge and no obligation.

https://books2read.com/r/B-A-JXD-PXORB

BOOKS 2 READ

Connecting independent readers to independent writers.

Did you love *The Rumball Rumba: A Dickens Holiday Romance*? Then you should read *The Winterland Waltz A Dickens Holiday Romance*[1] by Bonnie Edwards!

[2]

In the quaint Christmas town of Dickens love will find a way...

When Kayley James learns she's the "other woman," she retreats to Dickens distraught. She needs an apartment, a job, and a touch of Dickens Christmas magic to get back on track and trust men again.

Nathan Brent, her new landlord, has secrets he can't share. As his friendship with Kayley blossoms into thoughts of forever, he scrambles to clear up past mistakes before she learns his ugly truth. Nathan has a long-lost Vegas bride and she's just shown up in Dickens with blackmail on her mind.

Approx: 195 pages

1. https://books2read.com/u/4jqR0Z

2. https://books2read.com/u/4jqR0Z

Read more at https://www.bonnieedwards.com/.

About the Author

Bonnie Edwards has been writing all her life, starting with a poem about Santa suffering with gout. She was seven, Santa was a thousandteen years old. Delighted with writing, she went on to write family sagas, humorous contemporary romance, romantic suspense and more.

Published by Kensington Books, Harlequin Books, Carina Press, and Robinson (UK) Bonnie's stories stretch from short stories to novellas and novels. Now, she's happy publishing her work herself.

With 40+ titles to her credit, she has been translated into several languages and sold books worldwide. Aside from standalone romances, she has multiple romance series that include Christmas romances and beach reads.

Contemporary family sagas find a home in Return to Welcome. Learn about more exciting releases and get a **free** romance by subscribing to her newsletter, Bonnie's Newsy Bits through her website.

Cheers and happy reading!

Bonnie Edwards

Follow her online: Amazon Website_BookBub_Twitter_Facebook Instagram

Read more at https://www.bonnieedwards.com/.